WRONG PERCEPTION

WRONG PERCEPTION

Based on a True Story

*Celeste —
Thanks for the support!*

James D. Jackson, Ph.D.

Pentland Press, Inc.
England · USA · Scotland

Wrong Perception is based on a true story. While the characters are actual people, their names have been changed to protect their privacy.

PUBLISHED BY PENTLAND PRESS, INC.
5122 Bur Oak Circle, Raleigh, North Carolina 27612
United States of America
919-782-0281

ISBN 1-57197-180-7
Library of Congress Catalog Card Number 99-070726

Copyright © 1999 James D. Jackson
All rights reserved, which includes the right to reproduce this book or portions thereof in any form whatsoever except as provided by the U.S. Copyright Law.

Printed in the United States of America

This book is dedicated to the memory of my grandparents James B. Jackson and Juanita Lawton Jackson, my daughter Brittini Ellen Jackson and my cousin Byron Grier.

Table of Contents

Foreword ix

Acknowledgment xi

Introduction xiii

The Lawton Family 1

Jones Family Crisis 27

The Maynard Family 43

Ronella and Byron 53

The Start of a Beautiful Friendship 65

Middle School Years 73

Glory Days of High School 79

Choices 101

Marriage, Lies, and Military 117

Desert Shield/Desert Storm 137

Gaining Confidence 147

Broken Promises 153

The Arrest 163

A New Beginning 173

Foreword

Wrong Perception is written in the tradition of the great American novel. It is a true-life drama that eloquently captures the lives of a close-knit group of people and examines their experiences, their relationships, the choices they made, and the consequences of those choices. *Wrong Perception* captures the very essence of the "American Spirit" by proving that self-actualization can be achieved by demonstrating the intestinal fortitude to overcome seemingly insurmountable obstacles. More importantly, *Wrong Perception* is one of the most inspirational stories written in this decade; it is a must read for all Americans.

Having known Dr. Jackson for some time now, I have seen this truly professional U.S. Army Officer at his best. This novel is merely a testament to his many talents and abilities. Dr. Jackson shares his most personal experiences with the reader, his innermost emotions are opened and explored. Through his unselfish and brutally honest depiction of the walk of life, its challenges and road blocks, it tragedies and failures, and the indomitable perseverance of the human spirit, Dr. Jackson provides the reader the greatest inspirational gift: hope.

The story begins in Atlanta, Georgia and extends as far as the Middle East. It centers around the lives of three friends, James, Reginald and Stacy. The story spans from their youth to their adulthood. It is a story of poverty and affluence, love and hate, life and death, marriage and divorce, and joy and tragedy.

The most compelling aspect of *Wrong Perception* is that the reader will personally identify with the characters, their lives and events. Dr. Jackson has come into his own as a writer. His characters are so real and so well developed that the reader will feel a personal connection with them. The events are so well described that the reader will actually become part of the scene.

Wrong Perception reaches into the depths of the human spirit, accentuating the fact that each individual controls his own destiny. Masterfully written with pinpoint accuracy, the novel stimulates the widest range of emotions. This thriller will make you happy, sad, angry, somber and excited. Most importantly, it will make you proud; and it will provide hope and inspiration to people from all walks of life. You will not have to look far to find this book, but you will have to look far to find another like it. It has taken Dr. Jackson four years to write this novel, and it is already on its way to becoming an American classic. And in the timeless tradition of the American classic, it will be read and re-read for many years to come.

Keith D. Shadrick
Captain, U.S. Army

First, I would like to thank my wife Sherrie and my daughters Jamie and Jessica for all of their love and support. Secondly, to my mother Yolanda Phillips and father Denis Jackson, thanks for giving me life and the opportunity to share this story with the world. I would also like to thank my good friends: Laral Milton, Byron German, Joseph Austin, James Kimble, Fredrick Anderson, Kenneth M. Chatman, Eric Whiters and Brandon Johnson for their ideas and true friendship. To my cousin Duane Grier, thanks for all of your words of encouragement. I would also like to thank Alloceia L. Hall and Christy Schuman.

This book was written in tribute to all of the young men and women who have overcome insurmountable obstacles. The story's inception is in Atlanta, Georgia and extends as far as Southwest Asia. The purpose of this book is to show that adversity is necessary to reach self-actualization. I have researched and observed many lifestyles, and I am certain that this story will impress any reader. This book was originally intended for my family, but after a few of my friends read the story and responded so optimistically, I decided to share it with the world. Enjoy.

Thank you,
James D. Jackson

1

The Lawton Family

James Lawton, a native of Augusta, Georgia, was not an educated man as far as formal schooling, but was very knowledgeable when it came to the ways of the world. When he finished the third grade, his father made him work on the farm to sustain the family and did not allow him to go back to school. Even as a young boy, family came first to James. He never once fought with his two younger sisters or younger brother. Lawton, as they called him, grew to be a very attractive man standing six-feet-tall with a slender but very muscular build. He had wavy dark brown hair that complimented his caramel brown complexion. Lawton built a reputation in Augusta as a hard working, kind, and considerate man. All the women in Augusta wanted the honor of being with a man of his looks and caliber. The only person that seemed to turn Lawton's head was the beautiful Julie Jackson. Julie stood 5'5" with curves in all the right places. She had a cocoa brown complexion, thick black curly hair that barely reached her shoulders and deep brown eyes that seemed to hypnotize every man in town. The only problem Julie had was that she was short tempered and harbored a lot of angry feelings for her mother who use to spank her at the drop of a hat. Julie was the oldest of nine siblings, and whenever Julie's mother and father would go out, they would leave Julie in charge. Whenever her siblings disobeyed her, she would spank them. Julie learned how to knit and sew from her grandmother. Julie started making clothes for her siblings as early as fourteen years old. She spent a lot of time by herself as a young teenager and would often talk about leaving home to get away from her mother. She was also the envy of every woman in town, since Lawton had eyes for her. After he finally got over his nervousness, he asked Julie for her telephone number, and she gave it to him without hesitation. He decided to call and ask her to the dance on Friday night at the local jazz club. The telephone was on its third ring when Lawton started to hang up. Suddenly he heard a soft voice on the other end of the telephone say "Hello, Jackson residence."

Being startled that someone answered, Lawton said in a slightly high pitched voice, "Yes, may I please speak to Julie?"

"This is she, may I ask who's calling," Julie stated.

Clearing his throat and speaking in his normal deep, sexy voice, "This is James Lawton, I was just wondering—"

Before James could finish his sentence, Julie interrupted and said, "Yes, Mr. Lawton, I know who you are. What can I do for you?"

"I would like for you to do me the honor of escorting you to the dance on Friday night," said the nervous Lawton.

"Why Mr. Lawton, you could have your pick of any woman, why me?" Julie asked.

"Because you are the most beautiful woman I have ever laid eyes on, that's why. So please be my date for Friday night, I promise you won't be disappointed," Lawton said.

"Okay, James, I'll go with you to the dance. Pick me up at 8:30 sharp," Julie said.

"Eight-thirty sharp it is, I'll see you Friday," Lawton answered.

Both hung up very excited and nervous about the long anticipated date.

On Friday, Lawton was there as scheduled to pick up Julie. As he approached Julie's door, he could feel the sweat building on his forehead. Lawton rang the doorbell and waited for someone to answer. In his right hand he held a single red rose behind his back. He was dressed in a blue "zoot" suit with white pin strips, a white shirt, a pair of black Stacy Adams and a white wide brim hat. When Julie answered the door, her heart skipped a beat at the sight of this gorgeous Adonis that stood before her. Julie was dressed in a pale blue power dress that fit her body like a glove. It was cut low in the front, but did not reveal too much. However, it was very sexy nonetheless. The dress was knee length and Julie wore flesh tone stockings with black pumps. When James saw Julie, he knew he was struck by Cupid's arrow.

"Good evening, Julie," Lawton said while handing her the rose and bowing to greet her. "A beautiful flower for a beautiful lady."

"Why, thank you, Lawton, you look nice yourself," Julie said as she bit her lower lip.

"Well, we ought to be going, everyone should be getting there right about now," Lawton said as he reached for her hand.

"Let me grab my wrap and then I'll be ready to go," Julie said.

Lawton opened the passenger door of his navy blue 1934 Chrysler Airflow and waited for Julie to get in. He then went around the car and got in on the driver's side and the two were off to the jazz club. Once at the club, everyone inside was dancing to the sounds of Duke Ellington's "Mood Indigo." When Lawton and Julie got on the dance floor, they were the epitome of grace and elegance. They practically cleared the floor as the other club goers looked on with amazement. The couple danced all night to the sounds of Billie Holiday, Benny Goodman, Glenn Miller and Bessie Smith. By the end of the night, the two knew that they were in love. They continued to date exclusively for the next six months before Lawton asked Julie for her hand in marriage.

Once married, they moved to Patterson, New Jersey. In the 1940s many families moved North in order to find higher paying jobs, and to leave the discriminatory practices of the South. In order to work in the factories in the north, one did not need a copious education. Yet, the factories provided Julie and Lawton with a sufficient enough income to buy a home and to raise a family. Julie stopped working in the factories when she became pregnant with their first child. In November of 1944, Julie gave birth to a baby girl that they named Carolyn. Six years later she gave birth to a boy, Marcus. Julie was the parent that disciplined the children. Lawton on the other hand, wanted to talk to Carolyn and Marcus to see if they knew the difference between right and wrong. Of course, Julie did not like for Lawton to be around when the children did anything wrong, because when he was around he would not let her beat their children. When their father was not home and Carolyn and Marcus did anything that

Julie did not agree with, the two were terribly beaten. Carolyn and Marcus had a very loving relationship with their father. Their relationship with their mother on the other hand suffered tremendously. Although Julie loved her children very much, they had a difficult time believing that she loved them at all because she was so strict. She wanted the best for them in the sense of personal relationships, education and material things. Julie made sure that Carolyn and Marcus attended the best public schools, even if she had to drive them twenty miles to get them there, and she would make or buy her children the most fashionable clothes possible.

Carolyn was not very happy about living in the North and could not wait until she was old enough to leave what she thought was a God forsaken place. Carolyn tried to make the best of her childhood. Her mother placed her in singing lessons and Carolyn did find a sense of peace during her lessons. With the help of her instructor, Carolyn's voice developed into that of a beautiful mocking bird. Just as Carolyn wished, the years seemed to fly by and the time had arrived for her to start thinking about college. Her parents did not want their daughter to go out of state for school, but this was Carolyn's opportunity to break free from the physical and emotional abuse of her mother. During the summer of her junior year in high school, Carolyn started applying for colleges out of state and was accepted at Fisk University in Tennessee. Carolyn seemed to float through her senior year of high school, because she knew the time was nearing for her to go away. Although her parents hated to see her go, they decided that they would not hinder her education like their parents did them.

The big day had finally arrived. Carolyn was in her room packing her clothes to attend Fisk University when her father appeared at her door. He startled her when he knocked on the door.

"Hi, baby girl, is there anything I can help you with?" Lawton asked.

"Hi, Daddy. No, I am almost finished. I will need your help when it's time to take my suitcases downstairs," Carolyn said.

"Can I talk to you for a minute, baby girl?" Lawton asked.

"Sure, Daddy, what's wrong?" Carolyn asked.

"Nothing," Lawton said as he headed to the chair at Carolyn's desk to sit down. "I'm just going to miss my baby girl that's all," Lawton said.

"I am going to miss you too, Daddy," Carolyn said as she raised her head from packing and looked into her father's tearful eyes.

It was at that moment that Carolyn saw tears fall from her father's eyes and rolled down his cheeks. She had never seen her father cry before. To Carolyn, Lawton was the type of father that was fair, but stern with her and her brother. He always hugged, kissed and told his children that he loved them, but never did he cry. Carolyn dropped the red and blue plaid skirt that she was folding on top of the other folded clothes in the truck, ran and threw her arms around her father's neck. She pressed her face so tightly against her father's face that you could not tell where his tears started and hers ended. The two of them cried and held each other for a minute before Lawton was able to speak. Carolyn finally let go of her father's neck and moved some of the clothes that covered her bed to the floor so that she could sit down and give her father her undivided attention. Lawton wiped the tears from his face and eyes and cleared his throat, but still spoke in a soft voice.

"Carolyn, I know there comes a time when parents have to let their children go and spread their wings to be the best that they can be. Baby, what I'm trying to tell you is that I'm proud of you," Lawton said.

"Thank you, Daddy," Carolyn said as a tear rolled down her round cheeks.

"Carolyn, your mother and I did the best we could to raise you to be a healthy happy person," Lawton said, pausing for a moment before going on. By this time, Carolyn was holding her head down looking at the floor. "Baby girl, look at me please, I know that your mother and I were not the best parents always, but we do love you, never forget that. If you ever need us we will be here for you," Lawton said.

Carolyn gave a small sigh before speaking, "Daddy, I know that you and mom did your best and I'm grateful to you both, but it's time for me to leave," Carolyn said as her eyes scanned the room and came back to her father's eyes for his reaction to her statement.

Lawton got up from the chair and said in a very low voice "You're right, baby girl, the time has come, now give your old dad a hug so you can get back to your packing."

"You are far from being old, Daddy," Carolyn said as she stood up to give her father a tight hug around his neck.

"I love you, baby girl," Lawton whispered in her ear.

"I love you too, Daddy," Carolyn whispered back.

"Now you get back to work," Lawton said as he headed for the door.

"I will Daddy," Carolyn said giving a slight wave to her father on his way out the door. Once Lawton left the room Carolyn sat back on the bed and realized that she was truly going to miss her father. After about ten minutes of crying her eyes out, Carolyn decided to turn on the small radio that sat on her desk to cheer up her gloomy mood. The radio was set on her favorite station, WRXB 105.5. Once the sounds of Smokey Robinson filled the room, Carolyn broke the depressed mood that she was in and began dancing and singing around the room while packing the rest of her belongings. Just as Carolyn finished packing and closed her last suitcase, there was another knock on her door. She looked up, and to her surprise, it was her younger brother Marcus standing there.

"What do you want, Marcus?" Carolyn said in a snapping voice. It was because of Marcus that Carolyn stayed in trouble with her mother.

"I don't want ya, but Mama does!" Marcus snapped back as he turned to leave and slammed the door behind him.

"Oh, great, what now?" Carolyn said to herself as she headed towards her bedroom door to go downstairs to see what her mother wanted. As Carolyn headed down the stairs leading to the dining room, she could smell the wonderful aroma of her mother's fried chicken, collard greens, sweet potato pie, macaroni and cheese and pan-fried corn bread. When Carolyn finally got to the end of the stairs and turned the corner into the dining room, there was Julie, Lawton and Marcus screaming to the top of their voices "Surprise!" Carolyn was truly shocked to see that her family went to so much trouble.

"You shouldn't have," Carolyn said as she could feel the tears well up in her eyes, but luckily they didn't fall.

"You know I had to do something special for my baby," Julie said as she motioned everyone to sit down at the dinner table.

"Thank you, Mama, everything looks so good," Carolyn said as she reached for the chair to sit down.

Everyone sat down and joined hands and waited for Lawton to say grace. With all heads bowed, Lawton began the grace "Thank you, Lord, for this food we are about to receive for the nourishment of our bodies. Thank the hands that prepared this food, Lord, so that we may continue to grow healthy and strong and do your will, Lord. Also, Lord, watch over my baby girl as she goes off to school," Lawton said as everyone joined in with "Amen!" Everyone was quiet during the course of dinner. Once everyone finished dinner Julie reached under the table and pulled out this big box wrapped in gold wrapping with a bright red ribbon and bow.

"Here baby," Julie said as she handed the box to Lawton to pass to Carolyn.

"What is this? It's not my birthday or Christmas," Carolyn said as she took the box from Lawton.

"You know we couldn't send you off without a gift for our college girl," Julie said. Julie was the best seamstress around the neighborhood. She had made Carolyn a gray blazer with a matching skirt that came just above the knee and a blue pantsuit to add to her wardrobe. Carolyn's eyes widened like a little kid on Christmas morning as she tore the bow and wrapping off the box, being careful not to tear the ribbon so that she could use it later for her hair. When Carolyn saw the two outfits her mother made her, she rushed from her chair to give her mother and father a hug. She was in such a good mood, she even hugged her little brother.

"Thank you Mama, they're beautiful!" Carolyn said as she held the outfits close to her heart.

"Now, you go on up stairs and try your clothes on to make sure they fit," Julie said. Before Julie could finish her sentence, Carolyn was halfway up the steps. Once in her room, Carolyn decided to try on the blue pantsuit first to see if it fit. She looked in the mirror, and realized that she was now a woman who had grown from that awkward little girl with the two pigtails, to a stunning young woman. She stood 5'4" with thick light brown shoulder-length hair, a caramel complexion like her father, and the figure of a goddess. Carolyn was finally happy with her body and she loved the way the pantsuit complimented her figure. Next, she tried on the gray blazer and matching skirt. She liked the way it fit, but liked the pantsuit better. She decided to leave out the pantsuit to wear the following day for her first day at Fisk University. Carolyn wanted to make a big impression on the other students. Just as Carolyn was putting back on her white shorts and blue tee shirt, there was a knock at her door.

"Come in," she said as she started folding up the gray blazer and skirt to put with the rest of her clothes in the trunk.

"How did the clothes fit, honey?" Julie asked as she stood in the doorway.

"Everything fit fine, Mama, thanks again for everything," Carolyn said as she went to give her mother a hug. Julie gave Carolyn such a weak and dry hug, that Carolyn pulled away quickly from her mother.

"Well, you better be getting ready for bed you have a big day ahead of you tomorrow," Julie said as she turned to go back down stairs to clean the kitchen.

"Okay," Carolyn said in a low whisper. She went over to her dresser to get her nightgown, panties and robe, so that she could take a warm bubble bath. The bathroom was located just across the hall from her room. Carolyn locked the door behind her because Marcus had a tendency to burst in the bathroom on occasion when she was in the middle of taking off her clothes. Feeling safe, Carolyn began to take off her clothes. Once everything was off, she stood in front of the mirror staring at her nude body. She reached under the cabinet to retrieve the bubble bath then sat on the toilet as she turned on the water for her bath. She let the water run until the bubbles reached the top of the tub. Carolyn eased her way into the tub, being careful not to get any water on the floor, because her mother would have a fit if she did. This was exactly what she needed, a hot bubble bath. Before she knew it, she was day dreaming about her days on campus and being able to make her own decisions. When Carolyn finished day dreaming and all of the bubbles in the tub had disappeared, that was her cue to get out of the tub and towel off. Carolyn put on her white panties, pink nightgown with little white flowers, and her pink and white robe. Carolyn decided to roll up her hair before going to bed, because she wanted to look her best on her first day of being a "Fisk Fox." With twelve big hair rollers arrayed over her head, Carolyn went to tell her parents goodnight before turning in. Her parents were downstairs in the family room watching the small black and white television that sat on a small stand. Carolyn stood in the door of the family room and watched her parents, thinking how much she was going to miss them, while at the same time excited to soon be free.

"Goodnight," Carolyn said.

Both Julie and Lawton said at the same time, "Okay, baby, goodnight, sleep well."

Carolyn headed back up stairs for a good night's sleep. The alarm went off at 6:30 sharp the next morning and she sprung from her bed in a very cheerful mood, nothing could spoil this moment. She made her bed and dashed for the bathroom to wash up before getting dressed. While in the bathroom, Carolyn also removed the rollers from her hair to see if any curls set in over night. Her hair was usually hard to curl but this time there were curls. She thought to herself, *This is going to be a good day, my hair is full of pretty curls, and I am going away*. Carolyn rushed back to her room to get dressed. After getting dressed and fixing her hair, Carolyn headed downstairs. Her parents were already in the kitchen. Julie was cooking breakfast and Lawton was sitting at the table staring out the back door day dreaming. Carolyn with a wide smile on her face ran into the kitchen, "Good morning," she said heading to the small kitchen table to sit down.

"Good morning," Lawton and Julie said somewhat sadly.

"Baby, are you ready for me to bring your things down?" Lawton asked.

"Sure, Daddy, everything is by my bedroom door," she said.

Lawton got up and headed up stairs to get Carolyn's suitcases and other bags so that he could pack the car. The family was driving Carolyn to Tennessee immediately after breakfast.

Julie was just finishing cooking when Marcus ran into the kitchen, and ran his hands through Carolyn's hair. Carolyn grabbed Marcus's hand and pushed him away from her. Marcus yelled "Mama! Tell Carolyn to stop."

"Carolyn, this is your last morning. Leave your brother alone," Julie said in a sharp tone.

"But I didn't do any—"

Before Carolyn could finish her sentence, "Both of you stop it and eat your breakfast!" Julie exclaimed.

Just as Marcus sat down at the table, he stuck his tongue out at Carolyn. Carolyn, not in the mood for playing, rolled her eyes at her little brother. Julie already had the toast, grape jelly, bacon, and eggs on the table. Julie started calling for Lawton to come to the kitchen so that they could all eat breakfast. Julie sat the butter on the table and then started putting grits on the plates. They heard the front door close, and Lawton appeared in the doorway of the kitchen wiping his forehead with the sleeve of his shirt. Julie and Lawton sat down at the same time and they all joined hands and said grace silently.

After breakfast, all of them headed to the car for the long trip. Julie was the last one out of the house, she was carrying a basket filled with leftover fried chicken and sweet potato pie so they could snack on the trip. Carolyn prayed that the trip would go by fast, and it did. The family sang songs the entire trip. While everyone else was singing, Lawton yelled, "We're here!" They all stopped singing to look up and see a huge campus with hundreds of students and parents walking around trying to get their daughters settled in. When Carolyn got out of the car, she noticed three guys leaning against a tree looking at all the newcomers. One of the guys really caught Carolyn's attention. He stood 5'8" with dark wavy hair, a high yellow complexion and a thin mustache that gave him the most sexy lips. He obviously worked out with weights because he had a very muscular physique. He was dressed in a dark yellow shirt that complimented his complexion well, a pair of Levi's, and a pair of brown loafers. Just when he noticed Carolyn looking at him, she turned her head in the opposite direction. Carolyn pulled the paper out of her pocket that told her what building and room

Wrong Perception

number she would be staying in. "What building are you staying in Carolyn?" Julie asked.

"Building 101, room 211, Mama," Carolyn said as she pointed to the building off to the right. Her father and brother were already getting Carolyn's things out of the trunk of the car and waiting for further instructions as to where to go. Carolyn and her mother moved to the rear of the car to help with some of the bags, when Michael Jones, a medical student attending Meharry Medical school across the street, came over to offer his assistance with the bags. Carolyn was surprised to see the guy that was standing over by the tree, standing before her.

"Hi, my name is Michael, can I help you with your bags?" Michael asked as he flashed Carolyn his pearly whites.

"Sure son, we could use your help, you know how women pack. By the way, nice to meet you, Michael. Call me Lawton, everyone else does," Lawton said as he extended his hand.

"We really don't need any help," Julie said as she cut her eyes at Michael.

"What do you mean we don't need this young man's help? You don't have to carry these heavy suitcases," Lawton said as he looked at Julie.

"Fine Lawton, have it your way!" Julie said as she cut her eyes back in Michael's direction.

"If I'm interfering or intruding, please let me know," Michael said as he looked in Carolyn's direction.

"No, you're not intruding son, you'll have to excuse my wife. We just had a long ride that's all," Lawton said as he glanced at Julie.

"Hi Michael, I'm Carolyn," Carolyn said quickly before her mother could say anything.

"Nice to meet you, Carolyn," Michael said as he extended his hand to her. She shook Michael's hand and noticed how strong and soft they were.

"Well, we better be getting your stuff up to your room," Julie said in order to break up what was going on between Carolyn and Michael. Michael finally let go of Carolyn's hand, grabbed two suitcases and waited for Lawton to grab the other two suitcases before heading towards the building. Carolyn, Julie, and Marcus grabbed the other bags that sat on the ground and followed Lawton and Michael to the building. They all reached the second floor and found the door to room 211 standing wide open. There was someone already in the room unpacking. Tanya Macklin, Carolyn's roommate was in the room unpacking. Tanya was the epitome of being a "Fisk Fox." Tanya stood 5'9", she had green eyes, long, wavy reddish brown hair, and a slender body. Carolyn knocked on the door before entering. Tanya looked up from unpacking to see Carolyn, her family, and Michael all standing in the doorway.

"Hi, you must be Carolyn. I'm Tanya Macklin. Nice to meet you," Tanya said as she walked over to shake Carolyn's hand.

"Nice to meet you Tanya," Carolyn said as she shook Tanya's hand. Everyone else said their greetings to Tanya and began to move Carolyn's belongings into the room. Once all of Carolyn's things were in place where she wanted them, her parents gave her a hug and said that it was time for them to leave. Carolyn walked her family and Michael downstairs to say their goodbyes. Carolyn and Michael continued to stand next to each other as her family drove out of sight.

Michael was from New Orleans, Louisiana. He was a Creole and damn proud of it. He traced his ancestry back to Morocco, the land of the Moors, "Black people." His mother often talked to him about his heritage, which motivated Michael to be the best he could be. History states that the Moors ruled France and were the kings and queens of France. Many migrated to New Orleans over three hundred years ago, and some of their descendants still live there today. Michael often bragged that he came from the best stock in the world.

"Carolyn, I know we just met, but will you go out with me?" Michael asked, as he looked deep into her eyes as if he was looking into the depths of her soul.

Carolyn was looking deeply back into Michael's eyes and answered, "Yes, I would be delighted to go out with you," Carolyn could not believe how this man had hypnotized her with his good looks and charm.

"Good, the schools are having a joint picnic this weekend and I would love to show up with the most beautiful girl on campus on my arm," Michael said with a big smile.

Carolyn just continued to look at Michael's beautiful light brown eyes and pearly white teeth that seemed to have her mesmerized. Julie never allowed Carolyn to date in high school, and Carolyn jumped at the chance to date such a handsome man.

"I'll give you a call tomorrow with the time of the picnic on Saturday, okay?" Michael asked.

"Okay, but I don't know what the hall phone number is to give to you," Carolyn said.

"Oh, don't worry, it's in the directory, and believe me if I can't find the number I'll be under your bedroom window pitching rocks to make the arrangements," Michael said with a chuckle. Both Carolyn and Michael started laughing.

"I'll be waiting for your call tomorrow," Carolyn said as she glanced into Michael's eyes again. "Well, I better be getting back up to my room," Carolyn said as she turned to go back to her dorm room. Michael watched Carolyn as she walked back towards her dorm and into the building. When Carolyn walked into the room, Tanya was still unpacking her clothes. Tanya looked up when the door opened and smiled when she saw her.

"So, was that your boyfriend? He's cute," Tanya said as she glanced at Carolyn.

"No, I just met Michael. He is a medical student over at Meharry," Carolyn said as she smiled to herself.

"A doctor, huh? Man you're lucky. I wish I could snag me a doctor," Tanya said.

"I haven't snagged him yet," Carolyn said as she laid back on her bed.

"Hey, do you want to take a walk around campus?" Tanya asked as she hung up her last dress.

"Sure, I would love to see the rest of the campus," Carolyn said as she got up from her bed. Tanya and Carolyn became friends quickly. They discussed their family life, their likes and dislikes, over dinner at the campus cafeteria. They talked and laughed all the way back to their dorm room. The next morning they both got up early so that they could eat breakfast at the campus cafeteria and to find their classes for the next day. Tanya saw an old girlfriend of hers from high school standing outside of the library. Carolyn excused herself after being introduced to the short red headed girl. Carolyn felt this would be the best time to go back to the dorm to see if Michael had called. When Carolyn reached her dorm, there was a note taped to the door. It was a message from Michael and it read, *Sorry I missed you, are we still on for Saturday? I'll call back around 1:30. I'll talk to you later, Michael.* Carolyn couldn't wait until 1:30 to hear Michael's voice. Carolyn decided to take a nap until Michael's call. The knock on the door scared Carolyn. She jumped up from the bed and headed to the door. Carolyn opened the door to see a short, heavy-set, gray-headed woman standing before her.

"Hi, I am Sara, the dorm mother, are you Carolyn?" Sara asked.

"Yes, I am," Carolyn said as she rubbed her eyes.

"Well, you have a phone call down in the lobby, some guy," Sara said as she turned to go back to the lobby.

"Thank you, Ms. Sara, I'll be there in a minute," Carolyn said as she slipped on her shoes. Carolyn was floating on air as she made her way to the lobby. The telephone was located on the wall next to a big desk were all visitors had to sign in and out. Carolyn reached for the telephone and heard the person on the other end singing. "Hello, this is Carolyn," Carolyn said as she laughed to herself about his singing.

"Hi, this is Michael. Did I disturb you?" Michael asked, being embarrassed about his singing.

"No, you didn't disturb me," Carolyn said smiling to herself.

"Well, are we still on for Saturday's picnic?" Michael asked hoping and praying that she had not changed her mind.

"Sure we are, what time are you coming to pick me up?" Carolyn asked.

"The picnic starts at noon, is 11:30 okay?" Michael asked waiting for an answer.

"Eleven-thirty is fine, I'll see you then, Michael," Carolyn said. Both of them hung up the telephone excited about their date for Saturday. The first few days of classes were long and tough for Carolyn. It was not like high school where she received all A's and B's. She couldn't wait until Saturday. Carolyn stayed up almost all of Friday night trying to decide on what to wear. She finally decided to wear her navy walking shorts and white and lime green striped tee shirt, and blue sandals. On Saturday

Wrong Perception

morning, Carolyn was up at 9:30 getting ready for her date with Michael. He was there to pick Carolyn up at exactly 11:30. He was dressed in a pair of blue jean shorts, a red oxford shirt, and tennis shoes. Michael had, in the back seat of his red 1958 Volkswagen, a picnic basket with fried chicken, French bread, cheese, grapes, strawberries, a bottle of sparkling grape juice, two wine glasses, and a long stem red rose. Michael called Carolyn from the lobby telephone to let her know he was there to pick her up. She told him she would be right down. She waited five minutes before going down so she wouldn't seem so eager. When Carolyn finally got to the lobby, she saw Michael staring out the window.

"Hello Michael, I hope I didn't keep you too long," Carolyn said as she walked towards him.

"No you didn't and believe me, you're worth waiting for," Michael said as he reached for Carolyn's hand.

Michael gently took Carolyn's hand and kissed it. Carolyn thought she would melt because he had the softest lips and she couldn't wait to feel them against hers. Michael opened the lobby door and the two made their way to his car. Michael opened the car door and helped Carolyn get in. Carolyn noticed the picnic basket on the back seat of the car and once Michael got in the car, she asked Michael what was in the basket. Michael told Carolyn that it was a surprise and that she would see soon enough. The picnic was being held at the local park that was five blocks up from the schools. When they arrived at the park, Michael got the picnic basket and went to the trunk of the car to retrieve the blanket for them to sit on. Michael found a spot under a shaded tree next to the duck pond to lie out the blanket. Carolyn and Michael were sitting near Carolyn's roommate Tanya and one of Michael's classmates Gary Homes. When Tanya saw Carolyn she smiled and winked at Carolyn in approval and Carolyn blushed and smiled back. The faculty had many activities for the student body to participate in: flag football, tennis, volleyball, softball and horseshoes. Michael and Carolyn decided not to participate in any of the activities because Carolyn didn't have the right kind of shoes in order to play any of the sports. Michael and Carolyn walked around the park hand and hand looking and cheering on the other students and faculty that were playing games. They were getting hungry so they went back to their blanket and basket to eat. Once they sat down Michael asked Carolyn to close her eyes and when she did, Michael placed the rose from the basket in her lap and softly kissed her lips. The kiss was so electrifying that it sent chills throughout Carolyn's body. When she finally opened her eyes, she saw the beautiful rose in her lap. Carolyn knew that she was falling in love for the first time in her life.

"This is a lovely lunch you packed for us, Michael," Carolyn said as she reached for a chicken leg.

"Oh, it's nothing, just a little something I threw together," Michael said as he gave Carolyn a wink. Michael poured himself and Carolyn a glass of sparkling grape juice. They ate their lunch with little conversation. After lunch and after a lot of the students started leaving, Michael suggested to Carolyn that they go back to his apartment. Michael told Carolyn that his roommate was out of town for the weekend, picking up a few items that he left behind. Carolyn agreed and the two were off to Michael's place. Michael opened the door to the apartment and when Carolyn walked in, she was shocked to see a nicely decorated place. There was a navy sofa in front of the window and a love seat off to the right of the sofa, a small coffee table in front of the sofa and a television on a stand against the back wall facing the sofa. There were family photos and black art covering the walls and a stereo next to the television. In one corner, there was a big glass vase filled halfway with blue and white marbles. On top of the marbles were blue artificial flowers. Michael took Carolyn's hand and led her to the sofa, and he went over to the stereo and put on some soft music. Michael excused himself and came back with wineglasses and a bottle of red wine. Carolyn was so nervous that she gulped the wine in one swallow. Michael sensing her nervousness took the glass from her hand and placed it on the coffee table. He then gently held Carolyn's face in his hands and kissed her lips. Carolyn, being taken over by the hormones, started unbuttoning Michael's shirt. After realizing what she had done, Carolyn jumped up from the sofa.

"What's wrong, Carolyn?" Michael asked as he stood up.

Wrong Perception

"I'm sorry, I don't know what came over me. I don't want you to think that I am easy or do this with everyone," Carolyn said as she held her head down.

"No, I don't think of you that way," Michael said as he held Carolyn tight in his arms. "We don't have to do anything if you don't want too. Carolyn, I really like you and if you want to wait, that's fine with me," Michael said as he continued to run his hands through Carolyn's hair.

Just as Carolyn felt Michael's strong hands caress her hair, she lifted her head and kissed him. Michael picked Carolyn up and laid her on the sofa.

"Carolyn, are you sure you want this?" Michael asked as he looked deeply into her eyes.

"Yes Michael, I'm sure I want you to be my first," Carolyn said as she smiled at him.

"Wait right here, and close your eyes, I'll be right back," Michael said as he went running around the apartment. Michael ran to the refrigerator to get the rest of the roses that he was going to give Carolyn later that night. He ran to his bedroom, folded the blanket and the sheets back, and put the rose petals all over the pillows and sheets. He then lit candles and set them on the nightstands and dresser. When the room was ready, Michael ran back in the living room to get Carolyn.

"Keep your eyes closed," Michael said as he held his hands over her eyes to make sure she didn't peek.

"Michael what are you doing?" Carolyn asked, while being led by Michael to his bedroom.

Michael finally stopped in the doorway of his room and took his hands from Carolyn's eyes. "You can open your eyes now," Michael said.

Carolyn opened her eyes and could not believe how beautiful the room was. Carolyn turned and threw her arms around Michael and kissed him. Michael gently picked Carolyn up, continued to kiss her and carried her to the bed. He laid her on the bed of rose petals, took off her tee shirt and bra, and tossed them to the floor. Michael, now over Carolyn, softly kissed and caressed her breasts with his tongue, and Carolyn moaned with pleasure. Michael slowly licked around Carolyn's left nipple and then her right. He licked his way to her midsection and then gently licked around her belly button and with one motion of Michael's hand he had Carolyn's shorts unbuttoned and unzipped. Michael pushed her shorts down just a little exposing her pubic hair. Carolyn was now slowly moving her head from side to side on the pillow and biting her bottom lip ever so slightly as ecstasy filled her entire body. Michael stopped to get the wineglass filled with red wine; he sipped a little and then poured some of the wine into Carolyn's belly button. Carolyn shivered as the cold wine chilled her silky skin. Michael placed the glass back on the nightstand and began to lick the wine from Carolyn's belly button. He licked until the sweet taste of the wine had disappeared and he now tasted Carolyn's own sweetness. Michael's strong but delicate hands gently lifted Carolyn's body up from the bed in order to remove her shorts and black panties. Michael paused for a brief moment to marvel at her exquisite body. Carolyn leaned up and kissed Michael with a very long and passionate kiss. Carolyn slowly took Michael's unbuttoned shirt off and flung it to the floor. Carolyn then slowly ran her hand across Michael's muscular chest and down across his shorts stopping right at his erect manhood. Michael began to unbutton his shorts as Carolyn massaged his manhood. While Michael took his shorts and boxers off, Carolyn laid back feeling excited and scared all at the same time. Her eyes widened at the sight of Michael's now exposed and erect manhood. Michael took his hands and placed them on her knees, Carolyn's body shivered at his touch. He parted her legs slightly and kissed Carolyn's knees and then her thighs. He took his tongue and licked from her inner right thigh to her never before explored womanhood. Carolyn let out a soft cry of pure delight. Michael could feel his manhood aching to explore every crevice of Carolyn's body. He kissed his way back up to Carolyn's beautiful face and slowly kissed her eyes, nose, cheeks, and lips lingering at each spot. He slowly and gently took his erect manhood and attempted to enter Carolyn's now throbbing womanhood. Carolyn screamed from the pain as Michael tried to enter her womanhood.

"Oh Michael that hurts, but I know I want to do this."

"Okay baby, let me get some lotion, maybe that will help," Michael said as he went to the bathroom and came back with the lotion.

After Michael applied the lotion to his manhood, he slowly tried to enter Carolyn again. This time the insertion was much better for Carolyn and the pain was tolerable.

Carolyn wrapped her arms and legs completely around Michael's body. With every thrust, Carolyn's body became more receptive to Michael and she began to moan with ecstasy. Michael continued until Carolyn reached an uncontrollable pleasure. Michael rolled along side of Carolyn and held her tight wanting to never let go. Carolyn buried her head into Michael's chest feeling safe and secure in his arms. She closed her eyes and drifted off to sleep. Michael ran his fingers through Carolyn's hair pushing it off her face, kissed her on her forehead, and the two drifted off to sleep. Michael woke up first and looked at the clock on the nightstand to see that it was 9 P.M. He kissed Carolyn on her lips and, like Sleeping Beauty, she opened her eyes to see Michael smiling at her.

"Are you all right, baby?" Michael asked as he got up from the bed and sat beside Carolyn.

"A little sore, but I'll be fine Michael," Carolyn said as she sat up on the bed. "What time is it?" Carolyn asked.

"It's 9:00," Michael said as he reached on the floor for his boxers to put on.

"I guess you better take me back to my room, curfew is at 10:00 P.M." Carolyn said as she reached for her clothes Michael was handing to her. Michael got up and made his way to the bathroom, that was located down the hall, he turned on the shower and yelled to Carolyn to come join him. Carolyn dropped her clothes on the bed and ran to the bathroom to join Michael. He was already in the shower and she quickly put her hair in a bun and jumped in the shower with him. Michael washed Carolyn from head to toe stopping in various places and kissing them. Once Michael was done, Carolyn did the same to Michael. They enjoyed the warm water and each other for a while before getting out. Both dried off and put their clothes back on. Michael and Carolyn held hands on the way to the car. Once in the car, Michael asked Carolyn, "When am I going to see you again?"

"Well, I'm not sure. I have a lot of reading and studying to do," Carolyn said as she glared out the window.

"What are you studying?" Michael asked as he reached over and touched Carolyn's hand.

"Greek and Roman literature, and it's Greek to me," Carolyn said.

"Well, maybe I could help you study?" Michael asked, smiling because he knew that this way he would be able to spend a lot of time with Carolyn.

"No, I don't want to take you away from your studies. I'll manage," Carolyn said as she smiled at Michael. "Just give me a call Wednesday and maybe we can make some plans for the weekend."

"I'll call you Wednesday then," Michael said as he pulled into the parking lot in front of Carolyn's dorm. Michael leaned over, caressed Carolyn's face, and kissed her now colorless lips. Carolyn got out of the car and made her way to the lobby door. Once inside she watched as Michael drove off.

Carolyn was busy every day trying to study for her classes. She almost forgot that Michael was going to call her on Wednesday. She did not have time to wait by the telephone because she had to go to the library. Carolyn did not leave the library until almost nine that night and she was sure that when she got back to her room, there would be a message from Michael. Carolyn was floating on air at the thought of Michael calling. When she reached her room, there was no note on the door. Carolyn heard noises coming from her room, so she thought Tanya put the note on her desk. "Hi Tanya, how did your studying go?" Carolyn asked as she made her way over to her desk to put her books down and to see if there was a message from Michael.

"It went as well as studying could go," Tanya said as she looked up from her history book with a grim look on her face.

"Well, I'm going to turn in," Carolyn said as she gathered her nightclothes and headed to the bathroom down the hall. While Carolyn was in the shower, her thoughts wondered to Michael and questions of why he didn't call haunted her. When Carolyn returned to the room, Tanya was already in the bed. Carolyn got

Wrong Perception

in the bed and went to sleep herself. The next day while Carolyn and some of her classmates were in the cafeteria eating lunch, Michael walked in with his roommate Ronnie Moore. When Michael saw Carolyn, he realized that he'd forgotten to call her. He was busy studying for a physics test that he had that morning. Michael made his way over to Carolyn's table.

"Hi, Carolyn, can I speak to you for a minute?" Michael asked as he motioned her to come outside.

"I'm kind of busy Michael, can I call you later?" Carolyn said cutting her eyes at him.

"Please Carolyn, it's important," Michael said as he held his hands in the praying position.

"All right, just for a minute. Excuse me everyone, I'll be right back," Carolyn said as she got up from the table and followed Michael outside.

Once they got outside, Michael tried to explain to Carolyn that the reason he didn't call was because he had a big physics test.

"Carolyn, I'm sorry. Let me make it up to you this weekend," Michael said with a puppy dog look on his face.

"I'm sorry too Michael, but I'm busy this weekend writing a term paper. If you had called me you would have known that," Carolyn said as she stared into Michael's eyes.

"Again I'm sorry that I didn't call, but I have to get through medical school for our future," Michael said as he gently rubbed Carolyn's face. Carolyn broke out into a big smile and threw her arms around Michael.

"Does this mean that I'm forgiven?" Michael asked as he leaned over and kissed Carolyn on the cheek.

"Yes, you're forgiven," Carolyn said as she hugged Michael. "Give me a call Monday and we'll get together for lunch one day next week," Carolyn said as she started to go back inside with the rest of her classmates.

"I'll call you Monday and I won't forget, even if I have to tattoo a memo on my forehead," Michael said as he laughed. Carolyn laughed and went back inside and finished with her study group.

Over the next couple of days, Carolyn wasn't feeling well and Tanya suggested that she should go to the clinic. Carolyn agreed and Tanya went along for moral support. At the clinic, Dr. Thomas wanted to do a complete physical. The nurse came in to draw blood and asked that Carolyn wait in the waiting area until the doctor was ready to see her again. The doctor came to get Carolyn about twenty minutes later and explained to her that he would not be able to give her any answers until the blood work came back. The results would take anywhere from three days to a week and that he would call her as soon as they came back. Carolyn and Tanya headed back to their dorm. Carolyn seemed only to get worst over the next few days and was not able to go to class. Michael called Carolyn to see how she was doing and to see if there was anything he could do. Carolyn insisted that she didn't need anything and didn't want him to come over because she didn't want him to see her like she was. Carolyn would never forget that Friday morning when there was a knock on the door and Sara was there to tell her that she had a telephone call from the local clinic. Carolyn slipped on her slippers and headed to the lobby. When she finally reached the lobby, there was one other girl in the lobby watching television. Carolyn picked up the telephone.

"Hello, this is Carolyn Lawton," Carolyn said as reached for a chair to sit down.

"Hello, Ms. Lawton, Dr. Thomas will be with you in a moment," the nurse said to Carolyn. Just then Carolyn heard a click and was put on hold. After a few minutes, there was a male voice on the line saying "Hello, Ms. Lawton, this is Dr. Thomas and I have the results of your blood work."

"Yes, Dr. Thomas what is it? What's wrong with me?" Carolyn asked with concern in her voice.

"Ms. Lawton, would you like for me to make you an appointment to come into the clinic?" Dr. Thomas questioned.

"No Dr. Thomas, please give me the results now," Carolyn said in a nervous tone.

"All right, Ms. Lawton. The results of your blood work show that you are pregnant," Dr. Thomas stated.

"I'm what! The results have to be wrong. I can't be," Carolyn said trying to fight back the tears.

Wrong Perception

"I'm sorry Ms. Lawton, the test results are correct. Would you like to come in to the clinic and talk to a counselor," Dr. Thomas suggested.

"No, Dr. Thomas, I'll be fine. Thank you," Carolyn said, still in shock from the news that she received. Carolyn was in a daze walking back to her room. She couldn't believe that the doctor told her she was having a baby. What was she going to tell Michael? When Carolyn got in her room, she laid down on the bed. As soon as her head hit the pillow she could feel the tears roll down the side of her face. Carolyn cried herself to sleep and didn't wake up until she heard the door close. It was Tanya coming back from her classes.

"Hi Carolyn, how are you feeling today?" Tanya asked as she walked over to her desk and put her books down.

Carolyn slowly sat up on the bed and cleared her throat before speaking. "The clinic called today with my results," Carolyn said, but was interrupted by Tanya before she could finish.

"So what do you have, the flu?" Tanya asked holding her hands over her mouth and nose as to cover up from the germs.

"Believe me, what I have is not contagious," Carolyn said as she began to cry.

"Carolyn, what's wrong? What did they say?" Tanya asked as she got up and went and sat next to Carolyn putting her arms around her.

"Tanya, I'm pregnant," Carolyn said as she started to cry harder.

"Is there anything I can do for you?" Tanya asked.

"Yes, can you call Michael and tell him that I need to see him," Carolyn said as she gave Tanya a hug.

"Sure, I'll call him for you, I'll be right back," Tanya said as she headed out the door.

Tanya headed to the lobby to call Michael and realized when she got there that she forgot to get his number from Carolyn, so she had to look it up in the school directory. She finally found the number and dialed it. The phone was on its fourth ring before anyone picked up, "Hello, Moore and Jones residence, this is Ronnie speaking, how may I direct your call?" Ronnie said waiting for a response.

"Hello, may I speak to Michael?" Tanya asked.

"Hold on while I get him," Ronnie said as he put the telephone down. A few seconds went by before someone picked up the telephone. "Hello, this is Michael."

"Hi, Michael, this is Tanya, Carolyn's roommate. I think you better get over here fast, Carolyn needs you," Tanya said.

"What's wrong did something happen to Carolyn?" Michael asked with heavy concern in his voice.

"I'll let Carolyn tell you what's wrong, you just hurry and get over here," Tanya said waiting for his response.

"I'll be right over, give me ten minutes," Michael said hanging up the telephone. When Michael pulled up in the parking lot and got out of the car Carolyn was walking in his direction. She had tissue in her hand and Michael could see that she had been crying.

"What's wrong, baby? Tanya called me and it sounded urgent," Michael said as he put his arm around Carolyn.

"Can we sit in your car? I need to talk to you," Carolyn said as she put her arm around Michael.

"Sure, baby, anything you want," Michael said as he opened the car door so Carolyn could get in. Michael ran to the other side of the car and got in. "Now, tell me what's wrong?" Michael said now giving his undivided attention to Carolyn.

"Michael, I don't know how to tell you this," Carolyn said starting to cry again.

"Whatever it is, we can get through it together," Michael said.

"All right, Michael, here it goes. We're going to have a baby," Carolyn said holding her head down and closing her eyes waiting for Michael to scream.

"Oh Carolyn, you've made me the happiest man alive," Michael said as he grabbed Carolyn and kissed her.

"What, you're not upset?" Carolyn said with a surprised look on her face.

"No, of course I'm not upset. I love you Carolyn, will you marry me?" Michael asked as he held Carolyn's hand.

"Oh Michael I love you too, and yes, I'll marry you," Carolyn said as she leaned over and hugged Michael. Michael drove over to his apartment so that he and Carolyn could make plans for their wedding. They decided that they would elope because Carolyn knew that her mother would not approve and Michael didn't have a close relationship with his family. On Saturday morning, Michael and Carolyn were married at the courthouse with Tanya and Ronnie there to support them. Once the school found out that the two of them were married and Carolyn was pregnant, she had to drop out. Carolyn moved in with Michael and Ronnie until Michael finished school. Carolyn wanted to call her parents and give them the news about the wedding and the baby, but Michael felt that they owed it to them to tell them in person. Michael was in his last quarter of school and was offered an internship in Atlanta, Georgia once he finished school. The plan was to stop to see Carolyn's parents on the move to Atlanta.

After Michael attended his graduation, Ronnie and Michael packed the car for the trip to see Carolyn's parents, and then on to Atlanta. Michael and Carolyn pulled up into Carolyn's parents driveway. Carolyn's parents were sitting on the porch when a car pulled into the driveway. They didn't know who it was until Carolyn got out of the car. Lawton got up from his chair, ran to give his baby girl a hug, and shook Michael's hand.

"So, you brought my baby girl home for a visit?" Lawton asked Michael.

"Yes sir, I did," Michael said.

"Hi Mama," Carolyn said as she stepped on the porch.

"Looks like you put on some weight there," Julie said as she cut her eyes at Michael and back to Carolyn.

"Can we go inside? We need to talk to you and Daddy," Carolyn asked.

All four of them went into the living room and sat down. Michael sat next to Carolyn and held her hand. Julie and Lawton sat on opposite ends off the sofa.

"Mom and Dad, Michael and I have something to tell you."

Before Carolyn could finish, Michael interrupted, "Carolyn, let me tell them. Mr. and Mrs. Lawton, I love your daughter and we have gotten married."

"You've what!" Julie said as she jumped up from the sofa and ran over and slapped Carolyn across her face. Michael jumped up and got in between Carolyn and her mother. Julie threw her hand back again this time to hit Michael, when she felt someone grab her hand. She turned around to see Lawton holding her arm.

"Let me go, Lawton!" Julie screamed to the top of her voice.

"No, you're not going to lay another hand on those children," Lawton said in a firm voice. "Now sit down," Lawton said as he slightly pushed Julie back towards the sofa. Julie did as Lawton said, she had never seen him like this before. Lawton went over to Carolyn and Michael, hugged them both, and congratulated them. Both Carolyn and Michael thanked him for supporting them. Michael went on to tell them that Carolyn was also pregnant and that they were moving to Atlanta. Julie was upset at the news, and got up without saying a word and went upstairs. "Just give her some time to digest what you've told her," Lawton said as he hugged them again. He couldn't wait to be a grandfather. "Are you two staying the night?" Lawton asked as he went back and sat on the sofa.

"No Daddy, we have a long drive ahead of us and we just wanted to tell you the news in person," Carolyn said as she stood up. Lawton said his good-byes to Carolyn and Michael. While Michael and Carolyn walked to the car, Carolyn turned around one last time to look at her father. He was standing on the porch and noticed her mother standing at the bedroom window. When her mother noticed Carolyn looking at her, she closed the curtains. Carolyn and Michael got in the car and drove off.

2

Jones Family Crisis

Once Carolyn and Michael got to Atlanta, everything seemed to be going perfect at first. Michael didn't want Carolyn to work and that was fine with her since she was now six months pregnant. Carolyn spent most of her time alone because Michael was at the hospital a lot. When she did see him, he always complained about her, the house, and the hospital. Carolyn did not keep herself up, the house was a mess, and the hospital was a nuisance. Michael didn't make it easy for Carolyn because he was the reason the house was such a mess. He would leave his clothes on the floor, shoes all over the house, and dishes everywhere. She would even find plates and dirty cups in the bathroom. This morning was going to be different. Carolyn spent all night cleaning the house until it was spotless. She got up early in order to cook Michael breakfast. When Michael walked in the door, he smelled the aroma of bacon, eggs, grits, hash browns and toast. Carolyn had everything ready to be put on the table. "Good morning honey, how was your night?" Carolyn asked as she went to give Michael a kiss.

"What was good about it, you didn't have to work all night," Michael said as he turned his head in order to avoid Carolyn's kiss.

"Well, breakfast is ready," Carolyn said as she started putting the food on the plates. They both ate breakfast without saying anything. Michael finished eating, got up from the table, leaving the plate for Carolyn to get and went into the bedroom, closing the door behind him. Carolyn continued to sit at the table feeling like a failure. She finally cleared off the table and cleaned the kitchen. Carolyn tried to go into the bedroom but found that the door was locked. Michael had never locked the door before, and she didn't want to knock, because she didn't want to have another argument with Michael. Carolyn laid on the sofa and drifted off to sleep. Michael started calling her name at the top of his voice, waking her.

"Carolyn, come here!" Michael screamed.

Carolyn thought to herself, *What in the hell does he want now?* Michael screamed again for Carolyn to come to him. Carolyn slowly got up from the sofa and headed to the bedroom. Carolyn turned the doorknob to find the door still locked.

"Michael, the door is locked," Carolyn said as she stood in front of the door with her arms folded. She could hear Michael getting out of the bed and walking over to the door. There was a click and the door opened. Michael was already on his way back to the bed when Carolyn walked in the room. Carolyn stood by the dresser as Michael got back in the bed.

"Carolyn, please come over here and let me talk to you," Michael said patting the bed where he wanted Carolyn to sit down. Carolyn walked over and sat on the bed next to Michael. "I know that I've been hard to get along with lately and you are not to blame. Things at the hospital have been tough. I don't know how to explain it to you, but the white doctors have it easy and the white male hospital administrators are making it rough for us black doctors. Racism and discrimination directed towards blacks is almost unbearable in the south. Don't get me wrong, racism is everywhere, but it is definitely worse in the south. Many of the black doctors that work at the hospital want me to speak on national television against the racial tension that exists for black doctors in the south. There is a young black man named Martin Luther King, Jr. who has been speaking on behalf of black people, and I am suppose to meet with him next week," Michael said.

"Don't you think that it will be dangerous to get involved in something like that?"

"It will definitely be dangerous, but I don't want my children to have to grow up in this type of hatred and degradation. If I don't take a stand with Martin Luther King, then who will?"

"Well, baby, I don't think it's a good idea. I think that you should get along with the white man the best you can and not try and be a hero," Carolyn said.

"Well, my mind is made up, I'm fighting for my children and my people, and I'm sorry if that upsets you."

"If this is really what you want to do, I will support you in any way that I can."

"Carolyn, I'm sorry for the way I have been treating you, but this racism keeps me under a lot of stress. I come from the best stock in the world, and I am not going to bow down to the ignorant white men that my ancestors educated! I promise to treat you better, because I do love you," Michael said as he lowered his head in shame.

"Michael, I love you too, and I hope things at the hospital get better for you and the other black doctors," Carolyn said as she lifted Michael's head and kissed him softly on the lips.

"Hey, I'm off tonight. Why don't I take my best girl out for dinner," Michael said flashing a big smile.

"I would love to have dinner with you, Dr. Jones," Carolyn said as she got off the bed and curtsied to Michael. The two of them laughed and got in the bed and held each other like old times.

Later that evening Michael and Carolyn got dressed to go to dinner. Carolyn wore her hunter green pantsuit. The shirt had a wide collar and big gold buttons down the front. She put on her green flats and had her hair in a French roll with gold dangling earrings that Michael gave her as a gift, just because. Michael wore his khaki slacks, a white shirt and his wool blazer with suede patches on the elbows. Michael didn't tell Carolyn were he was taking her, but she knew it had to be their favorite Italian restaurant. They both loved the place because of the good food and the live romantic music. Things from that night on only seemed to get better for Michael and Carolyn.

On January 12, 1965, Carolyn gave birth to a healthy, bouncing baby girl. Michael and Carolyn named their beautiful, curly headed little girl, Gina Lauren Jones. Life could not get any better for Carolyn and Michael. Michael was offered a full time position with the hospital making a salary of $7,200 a year, with great benefits and incentives after his internship was completed.

Carolyn enjoyed having lunch with the other wives, endless parties, and charity events that came with being a doctor's wife. However, eventually, Carolyn started to become bored with the lifestyle and wanted more for herself. Carolyn started hinting to Michael that she wanted to go back to school. Michael refused to listen to her, he wanted his wife at home with their child. Michael was afraid that if he didn't do something quick about Carolyn's crazy ideals about school, she would leave him. He couldn't tell her his true feelings of wanting his wife beautiful, pregnant, uneducated, and at home. So one night when Carolyn brought up the subject of school again, Michael started to come on to her sexually because he had been keeping up with her menstrual cycle and knew that she was ovulating. Carolyn on the other hand thought that this would be a way to get Michael to let her go back to school. Carolyn wasn't counting the days because she and Michael were always careful, and Michael always told her when it was a good time or not, and this night, Michael said it was okay. Three weeks later, Carolyn found out she was pregnant and she couldn't believe it. What was she going to do with two babies? She was still much a kid herself. Michael was thrilled because at least for the next nine months, school was out for Carolyn. Michael had gotten a maid to clean up the house for Carolyn, and he was trying to make this pregnancy as easy as possible for Carolyn. Carolyn wasn't happy about her situation, but when that little life inside of her started moving, she started to glow with pride. She figured that when the baby was old enough, she would be able to go back to school. On February 3, 1966, Carolyn gave birth to a beautiful baby boy. Michael and Carolyn name him Johnny Darrel Jones. Michael was so happy that they had a baby boy. He counted little Johnny's fingers and toes a million times to make sure they were all there. He was a perfect baby. Carolyn enjoyed being a mother because she never wanted for anything. Her children were happy, healthy and beautiful. The day before Carolyn was to get out of the hospital Julie showed up with a teddy bear in hand and Carolyn's brother Marcus.

"What are you doing here Mama, and where is Daddy?" Carolyn asked with a confused look on her face.

"Carolyn, I know that we have not been on speaking terms since that day you and Michael showed up at the house, but something has happened that I need to talk to you about," Julie said with concern in her voice.

"How did you know I was in the hospital, and where is Daddy? Did something happen to him?" Carolyn asked now sitting straight up in the bed.

"Your father told me that you were in the hospital. I knew that he kept in touch with you," Julie said, not looking at Carolyn.

"What do you want, Mother? The last time I saw you, you made it clear that you wanted nothing to do with me or my husband," Carolyn said in a snapping tone.

"Carolyn, I'm sorry. I want you back in my life. I need you more than ever," Julie said as a tear rolled down her face.

"Mom, what's happened?" Carolyn asked, now leaning towards her mother.

"Your father and I have gotten a divorce. Marcus and I are moving here so that we can be closer to you and the children. I want to start fresh with you and get to know my beautiful grandbabies," Julie said now holding Carolyn's hand.

"Mama, I'm sorry about you and Daddy. When I last spoke to him, he said nothing about the two of you splitting up," Carolyn said with tears racing down her face.

"Don't cry honey. Marcus and I are doing just fine. I found a house and we'll be moving in this afternoon," Julie said trying to force a smile on her face. Marcus sat quietly in the corner the entire time Julie visited with Carolyn. The three of them walked to the nursery to see little Johnny. Julie held her grandson for the first time and couldn't wait to see Gina. Julie promised that as soon as she and Marcus got the house in order, they would come out to Carolyn's home for a visit. After a nice reunion, Carolyn walked Julie and Marcus to the elevator, gave both of them a hug and a kiss on the cheek and said good-bye.

When Gina was twenty-one months old and Johnny was eight months old, Carolyn started getting those old urges of wanting to go back to school. On Friday night, Carolyn sent the children to the babysitter because she wanted to talk to Michael alone. Carolyn cooked a nice candle light dinner for two: T-bone steaks, baked potatoes, a tossed salad, hot yeast rolls, and bought a bottle of Chardonnay. For dessert, Carolyn made a creamy strawberry cheesecake. For a woman that had recently given birth to two children, Carolyn still looked like a model. She wore a long black sleek dress that showed her every curve. Her make-up was perfect, and her hair was up in a French roll with curls dangling down both sides of her face. Everything was perfect. Carolyn rushed over to the stereo to turn on some soft music. Michael was due home any minute and she wanted to be ready.

When Michael walked through the door minutes later, he yelled, "I'm home! Where is my beautiful family?"

"Hi baby, I'm in the dining room. Dinner is ready," Carolyn said yelling to Michael.

Michael walked into the dining room to find candles lit and dinner on the table.

"Dinner is served," Carolyn said as she pulled the chair out for Michael to sit down.

"Everything looks lovely, but where are the children?" Michael asked, looking around for the kids.

"The kids are at the babysitter's, tonight is our night," Carolyn said pouring Michael a glass of wine.

"What's the special occasion?" Michael asked as he reached for the steak sauce.

"I love my husband, is that occasion enough?" Carolyn asked smiling at Michael.

"Yes it is, and you look stunning," Michael said, flashing her his pearly whites.

"Thank you dear," Carolyn said smiling back at him.

They both enjoyed the food, the music, the wine and each other. After dinner Michael went over to Carolyn and extended his hand to her in order for them to dance. They danced so long, that they didn't realize that the music had stopped. Michael kissed Carolyn very passionately. "Michael, don't you want your dessert?" she asked when he pulled her towards the bedroom.

"You are my dessert," Michael said as he stopped and picked Carolyn up and carried her the rest of the way to the bedroom. They made love like it was their first time. There was excitement, passion, and tenderness during their sexual encounter. As they

Wrong Perception

lay side by side, Carolyn pondered how she would bring up the subject of her going back to school again.

"Michael, what would you think of me going back to school?" Carolyn asked as she cuddled up closer to Michael.

"Here we go again! Can't you get it through your thick skull that you are not going back to school as long as you're with me? Understand?" Michael said as he got up from the bed.

"Michael, why are you being so pigheaded? You are not the only one that can get educated you know," Carolyn said as she sat up on her knees.

"As long as I'm bringing home the paycheck, I'll be the only educated one in this house," Michael said as he walked out of the room.

Carolyn was so upset, that she grabbed the first thing in her reach. She grabbed a wineglass that was sitting on the nightstand and flung it at Michael's head. He was lucky that Carolyn had bad aim and the glass went zooming by his left ear. Michael ran back to where Carolyn was on the bed, and raised his hand in order to slap her.

"You do it and that will be the last time you hit me. I'll take you for everything you've got," Carolyn said as she pointed her finger in Michael's face.

"You'll try bitch, you'll try," Michael said as he walked out of the bedroom.

Carolyn heard the shower in the bathroom so she hurried up and threw on her jean dress that was draped on the back of the chair in their room. She decided to pick up Gina and Johnny from the babysitter although they were supposed to spend the night. She didn't know what to expect from Michael. Carolyn wanted her children with her, she thought that they were her protection from Michael. He wouldn't do anything with the children there. When Carolyn returned home with the children, Michael was sitting in a chair with his arm folded in front of the door.

"Where have you been?" Michael said before he saw the children.

"Daddy, Daddy," Gina screamed as she ran to Michael. Johnny was in Carolyn's arms and when he saw his father, he started crying to get down. Johnny could barely walk but he made it to Michael with open arms. Carolyn stood in the doorway and watched Michael with the children. He had both Gina and Johnny in his lap giving them a hug, but when he looked up at Carolyn, he gave her a stare that sent chills throughout her body. Carolyn made her way pass Michael and the children, and went into the bathroom to take a shower. When Carolyn felt that it was safe to come out, she got out of the shower, dried off and put on her long navy gown that hung behind the door. Carolyn looked first in their bedroom to see if Michael was in bed and when he wasn't there, Carolyn looked in the children's room and found Michael tucking the children in and settling down to read them a bed time story. Carolyn appreciated Michael being a good father and wished he could be more of a supportive husband. Neither Michael nor the children noticed Carolyn watching them, so she headed to the bedroom and anticipated Michael coming to bed. Michael finished the story, kissed the children on their little foreheads, turned the lights out, closed the door and headed to his bedroom. When Michael got to the bedroom Carolyn was in bed reading a brochure from Georgia State University. Michael ignored Carolyn because she was not going to spoil the good mood that the children put him in. Carolyn saw that Michael was not paying her any attention so she put the brochure on the nightstand and turned out the lights. They laid with their backs to each other and said nothing, not even goodnight.

    Over the next few weeks, Carolyn and Michael barely spoke to each other unless it had something to do with the children. All of a sudden, Carolyn started feeling sick to her stomach and she realized that her menstrual cycle was five days late. She thought she may be pregnant again just as she was really going to go back to school whether Michael liked it or not. Her concerns of being pregnant were confirmed and as the doctor told Carolyn the news, she sat in shock. Carolyn was in a daze for the rest of the day. She had to tell Michael the news, and she knew that he would be thrilled because this would end her thoughts of going back to school once again. Carolyn was in the kitchen with Ruby, the cook, when Michael came home from the hospital. Ruby was a very attractive older lady. She had straight silver hair that she always had pulled neatly back into a bun. She had a dark brown complexion, hazel eyes that sparked every time she spoke and was in good shape to be sixty-five years old. Michael placed his black bag on the counter and reached in the cabinet for a glass and in the refrigerator for some cold iced tea.

"Where are the children?" Michael asked.

"In their room playing until dinner," Carolyn said without raising her head to look at Michael. Michael left the room with his tea in his hand. He went to the children's room to see how they where doing. He stood in the doorway watching Gina show Johnny how to play tea party.

"How are Daddy's favorite children?" Michael asked as he stepped into the room.

"Daddy!" both Gina and Johnny yelled to the top of their voice, getting up from the small table, running to their father and grabbing him around his legs.

"Daddy, can I have some?" Gina said, pointing to Michael's glass.

"Sure baby," Michael said bending down to give Gina some tea. Johnny, wanting some too, started pulling on the glass.

"Stop, Johnny," Gina yelled, trying to push him.

"Wait son, I'll give you some," Michael said moving Johnny's hands away from the glass. Michael picked Johnny up and told Gina to follow him to the kitchen. Carolyn and Ruby were still preparing dinner when Michael and the children entered the kitchen like a herd of cows.

"Dinner is almost ready, so you and the children need to get washed up," Carolyn said as she was putting ice in the glasses.

"I'll wash the children up," Ruby said as she finished setting the table. Ruby grabbed both Gina and Johnny by the hand and led them to the bathroom to wash their faces and hands. Carolyn placed the glasses and the children's cups on the table, got the salad out of the refrigerator and tossed it one last time before putting some in a bowl. Michael sat at the counter and went through the daily mail without saying a word to Carolyn.

"Michael, I need to talk to you," Carolyn said.

"About what?" Michael asked.

"I'll talk to you after Ruby leaves," Carolyn said placing the bowl of salad on the table.

"If it's about school you can forget it," Michael said cutting his eyes at Carolyn.

"No, it's not about that, and I said I'll discuss it after Ruby leaves."

Ruby came back in the kitchen with the children and placed them in their seats. Carolyn got the plates out of the dishwasher and placed them on the table, while Ruby put some spaghetti and meatballs in a serving bowl. Ruby joined the Jones' for dinner, and once dinner was over, Ruby cleaned the kitchen and helped Carolyn bathe the children and put them to bed. Some nights Ruby stayed the night, but tonight she sensed tension between Carolyn and Michael so she said good night and was on her way home. After Carolyn saw Ruby leave, she checked the house and made sure all doors were locked and turned out all of the lights. Michael was already in bed.

"Michael, are you asleep?" Carolyn asked as she changed her clothes.

"No, I'm not, what do you want?" he asked turning over to face Carolyn.

"I told you that I needed to talk to you," Carolyn said as she climbed into bed.

"Well, talk!" Michael snapped.

"There's no easy way to tell you, so here it goes, we're going to have another baby," Carolyn blurted out waiting for a response. Michael said nothing.

"Michael, did you hear what I said? We're going to have another baby," she said again.

"I heard you the first time," Michael said with little emotion. Carolyn was speechless and turned over and tried to go to sleep. Michael's lack of emotion confused her. Was he happy, was he sad, did he want the baby or not? These were the thoughts that ran through Carolyn's mind all night long. The next morning Michael seemed to be in a different mood. He was happy about having another child and made sure he let Carolyn know it.

Eight and a half months later, on August 15, 1967, Carolyn gave birth to a beautiful baby boy. She named him without Michael's help. The baby reminded Carolyn so much of her father that she named the baby James Darren Jones. Little did she know that he would turn out to be more like his grandfather than she imagined. Life with three children wasn't easy for Carolyn and it was about to get harder. When James was seven months old, Carolyn found out that she was pregnant yet again and this time would be her last. She gave birth to another little boy on January 8, 1969 and named him Jeff Daniel Jones. After the birth of Jeff, Carolyn and Michael's marriage seemed to deteriorate.

"Carolyn, I am going to a National Association for the Advancement of Colored People (NAACP) meeting. I should be home about eleven o'clock tonight, so don't wait up. Martin Luther King, Maynard Jackson, who is a Louisiana Creole I might add, Julian Bond and Andrew Young are all supposed to be there. These guys are some of the smartest black men I have ever met in my life. The five of us are going to be speaking about the racial tension in the south and ways that we intend on improving things."

"Michael, you have been so involved with that association, that you don't spend much time with us anymore. Maybe I need to find something to do to occupy my time. I will see you when you get home," Carolyn said.

When Jeff was four months old, Carolyn started leaving the children at home with the babysitters for long periods of time. Most of the time Michael would beat Carolyn home and question the babysitter about Carolyn's whereabouts. Eventually, Michael started to accuse Carolyn of messing around or not supporting him in his idea of family. They would often get in shouting matches and Michael would end up calling her a "black male-castrating bitch." Little did Michael know, Carolyn had enrolled at Georgia State University. Carolyn would study late at night when the children were asleep and Michael was working nights at the hospital. One night after studying late Carolyn finally got in the bed around four-thirty in the morning and had just drifted off when Michael stormed in the room, demanding that she get up and cook him something to eat. Carolyn refused to move so Michael grabbed her by her arm and practically dragged her to the kitchen. Once they were in the kitchen Michael slung her into the refrigerator.

"Now get me something to eat!" Michael demanded.

Carolyn was crying and afraid to say or do anything because she didn't want to wake the children. Carolyn retrieved the hamburger from the refrigerator and a bowl from the cabinet. While Michael's back was turned, Carolyn poured Windex glass cleaner on the hamburger when she finished cooking it. When Michael took a bite of the hamburger, he nearly vomited at the taste.

"Carolyn, what in the hell is wrong with the hamburger?" Michael asked.

"I poured Windex on it you asshole!" Carolyn screamed.

Michael casually got up from the table and started walking towards Carolyn. "You stupid bitch," he said as he slapped her to the floor.

"That's it, I told you the first time you hit me would be your last, motherfucker," Carolyn said as she got up from the floor and rushed upstairs.

She ran into the bedroom were Michael kept his .45 caliber pistol, ran back into the kitchen where Michael was sitting and took a shot at him. Luckily, she missed. One of the Jones' neighbors heard the shot and called the police. Fortunately for Michael, he knew one of the arresting officers. Michael worked on the officer one night in the emergency room after a drug dealer stabbed the officer. Officer Thomason recognized Michael and pulled him to the side to see what was going on. Michael told the officer that he and Carolyn had a misunderstanding and the gun that Carolyn had accidentally fired. Officer Thomason asked to see the registration on the gun. Michael excused himself, went upstairs and within minutes was back with the papers. Carolyn was sitting on the sofa with the officer not saying a word because she wanted to know what Michael was telling the other officer before she said anything to get herself in trouble. Officer Thomason checked over the papers and told Michael that since he knew him that he would give him and Carolyn a warning. Michael was grateful to Officer Thomason. He was glad that a black officer showed up at the house. Before Officer Thomason left, he asked that one of them leave the house so that they may have a cool down period. Michael said that he was not leaving his house and the officers asked Carolyn if she had anywhere to go. Carolyn said that she had call her mother to make sure, and stated that if she left the house the children were going with her. Carolyn excused herself, went into the kitchen and called her mother. Carolyn explained that she and Michael had gotten into a fight and that she and the children needed a place to stay. Julie asked Carolyn if she and the children were okay, and told Carolyn that she and the children could stay with her as long as she needed to. She thanked her mother and told her that she and the children would be over in about an hour. Carolyn went back into the living room and approached Officer Thomason and told him that she needed to pack some things and get the children ready because she was going to her mother's house. Officer Thomason stated that he and the other officer would stay until she was ready to go to ensure that they made it safely out of the house. Carolyn thanked the officers and vanished upstairs to get the children ready and pack some clothes. She was back downstairs after about forty minutes with four crying children and two suitcases. The officers helped her put her bags in the car and tried to help get the children in the car, which was no easy task because they were screaming and crying while holding on to their father.

"Dr. Jones, please help us put the children in the car."

"Why should I help that bitch take my children? I love my children, and I could provide a better life for them," Michael said as he held Jeff in his arms while the other children hung on to his pants leg.

"Yeah, we will see who ends up with them and a nice chunk of your money asshole," Carolyn said as she pulled Gina off Michael's pant leg and put her in the car.

"Look, Dr. Jones, either you help get the children in the car or we'll make you leave the house, understand?" Officer Thomason said forcefully. Michael didn't say a word as he kissed Jeff on the cheek and gave him to the officer. Michael bent down and kissed James and Johnny on the cheeks, took them by their tiny hands and led them to Carolyn's car. The officer put the three boys in the car. Michael asked that he be able to kiss his children again. The officers agreed and Carolyn stood by and watched, not saying a word. Michael leaned in the car and kissed all four of his children, then sadly walked back to the house as the screams of his children rang in his ears. Michael didn't watch as Carolyn drove off. The officer left the scene after she drove away. Michael stood in the big house and cried. It was at that moment that he vowed to make Carolyn's life a living hell.

Two weeks passed before Michael was served with divorce papers. When the ugly and drawn out custody battle was over, the courts awarded Carolyn full custody of the children, and ordered that Michael pay $700 a month in child support. However, Michael lied and produced false papers about his finances and he was only ordered to pay $100 per child. Carolyn was outraged, but had no proof of Michael's real income. He never gave her access to the checkbooks and gave her a lump sum of $400 each week to spend.

Michael refused to pay child support because he knew that Carolyn would not be able to survive without it. Not for one minute did it cross his mind that the children would suffer without the money. Carolyn was only able to get a job making minimum wage. Carolyn was finally able to move out of her mother's home and get a house for her and the children. She had to lie in order to qualify for the house, but it was worth it. She and the children had a place to call their own. Although Michael was being a jerk, he still paid for the children to attend private school. Carolyn was barely making ends meet. Summer seemed to be better for Carolyn because her mother would watch the children for her and Carolyn didn't have to worry if her children were going hungry. August arrived and it was almost time for the children to return to school and Carolyn dreaded calling Michael for the money, but she had to call.

"Dr. Jones's office, may I help you," the voice on the line said.

"Hello, this is Mrs. Jones, is Michael in?" Carolyn said, waiting for an answer.

"Yes, hold on Mrs. Jones and he'll be right with you," the nurse said putting Carolyn on hold. *Oh, great he would be playing loud elevator music,* Carolyn thought to herself, pulling the phone away from her ear until she heard a living, breathing person.

"Yes, Carolyn, what do you want now?" Michael asked in a hurried tone.

Wrong Perception

"Well hello to you too, Michael," Carolyn said in a sarcastic tone.

"Cut out the games," Michael said angrily. "You want something, so what is it?"

"I was calling to see when you were going to give me the money for the kids' tuition. It is due in two weeks." Carolyn said.

"Sorry, Carolyn, but I'm not giving you the money anymore," Michael said.

"What do you mean you're not giving me the money? This is our kids' education we're talking about, Michael. I can't believe you're being so petty," Carolyn said, now getting upset.

"Well, you're working now and it's not in our divorce decree that I have to pay for private school," Michael said.

"Michael, you know damn well that I cannot afford to send three children to private school," Carolyn said, raising her voice a notch higher.

"That's too bad. The way I see it, you have two choices. Either give me the kids, or put them in public school," Michael said, feeling he had the upper hand. Carolyn slammed the telephone down in Michael's ear.

After that situation and others that occurred with Michael, Carolyn developed a bad habit of literally pulling her hair out. Michael sincerely believed that he should have been awarded custody of the children. In addition, he was hoping that Carolyn would fall on her face and give him the children because it would be too hard for her to raise four children with little or no money. This attitude landed him in jail on several occasions because he would intentionally not send Carolyn the child support for months. He knew the court wouldn't do anything until he was three months behind. After going to jail on several occasions, and losing money at his practice, Michael gave in and sent Carolyn the $400 dollars. Carolyn was not able to raise the money to send Gina, Johnny and James back to St. Paul's Academy, so she called her friend Pamela and asked her for the name of the best public school in Atlanta. Pamela told Carolyn that the best school to have the kids in was a school that was located on the north side of Atlanta, Barton Chapel Elementary. She told Carolyn that the school had the best to offer students without the private school cost. She also told Carolyn that everybody was trying to get their kid in that school. Carolyn made a few calls and was able to get a letter of reference from Calvin Long, Jeff's godfather and a good friend of Michael's. Calvin gave Carolyn the letter because he felt bad about the way his friend Michael was treating her. On Monday, Carolyn took the letter to Barton Chapel and was able to register the children for school a week before it started.

3

The Maynard Family

It was fall quarter and time for school to start again at Turner High School. Stefon Maynard was ready for his junior year, when his mother dropped him off at school. He was excited and thought that this was going to be his year. Over the summer, Stefon went through his growth spurt, and this year he was trying out for football. He knew he was good at football, but Coach Smith told him that he was too small to play during his freshman and sophomore years. Stefon was early, so he waited outside until some of the other students arrived. After his growth spurt, Stefon stood 5'9" and weighed 150 pounds. He had a flawless golden complexion, light brown eyes, curly hair and a smile that would make any girl's heart skip a beat. Busses started to pull up in the loading zones and the school grounds were soon crowded with students. Stefon saw his friend Deion get off the bus and he ran up behind him and slapped him on the back of the neck.

"Hey man, how was your summer?" Stefon asked.

"Man, look who's the big man on campus. What did you do, have somebody stretch you? I have to look up to you now," Deion said, holding his neck laughing.

"Aw man, cut it out," Stefon said, putting his notebook under his arm.

"So whose homeroom are you in this year?" Deion asked.

"I'm in Mr. Bailey's homeroom," Stefon said with a big smile on his face. Mr. Bailey was the coolest teacher to have at Turner High School.

"You lucky dog, you. I got that prune face Miss Bell, and I know that it is going to be hell." The two walked through the crowded hallways to their homerooms, which were across from each other. They said good-bye until lunch. Stefon walked into his classroom and decided to head to the back of the class, when he laid his eyes on the lovely Patty Jones. She was the first student to enter the classroom. All the other students waited to scrunch in during and after the bell rang. When Stefon saw Patty, he made a detour for the seat next to her. Patty was a new student at Turner High. She transferred from a school up north because her grandmother was sick and she and her mother were helping to take care of her. Mr. Bailey was asking Patty about the people and the school system up north, when Stefon plopped down in the seat next to her. Patty noticed Stefon when he came into the classroom, but didn't acknowledge his presence. Mr. Bailey welcomed all of the students and then covered the course agenda.

"Mr. Maynard? My have you grown over the summer, I almost didn't recognize you," Mr. Bailey said.

"Hello Patty, it is nice to meet you," Stefon said, flashing Patty his straight white teeth.

"It's nice to meet you too," she said, smiling back at Stefon.

"Well, if you don't have anyone to eat lunch with today, why don't you have lunch with me and my friend Deion?" Stefon asked.

"Thank you, Stefon. I would be more than happy to join you and your friend," Patty said now blushing.

Patty had a golden pancake complexion, with hazel eyes. She had high cheekbones and full lips. She stood 5'5" and weighed 108 pounds. Stefon couldn't take his eyes off Patty. Just when Stefon was going to say something to Patty the bell rung and the class was soon filled with students. The first thirty minutes of school were spent in homeroom where the roll was called and prayer was conducted. Mr. Bailey always started the class off with a joke and a funny story about his childhood. After his usual joke and story, Mr. Bailey introduced Patty to the rest of the class.

"Class, our new edition to Turner High, Patty Jones," Mr. Bailey said pointing to Patty.

Everyone at the same time said, "Hello, Patty." Patty just waved to the class. She could see that the girls were whispering, and the boys were all staring. The bell rang for everyone to go to

Wrong Perception

their first period class and everyone rushed out except Patty and Stefon. Patty was nervous about her first day. She was looking at her schedule trying to figure out which direction to go. Stefon picked up his notebook and asked Patty if she needed help locating her class. Patty gladly accepted and the two were off down the hall. Stefon showed Patty where all of her classes were and dashed off to his first class before the bell rang. Stefon didn't see Patty again until lunch time. He was sitting with Deion at the table they had occupied for the last two years in the back of the lunchroom when Patty walked in and stood in the lunch line. Patty was coming out of the lunch line when she heard her name being called. She spotted Stefon and headed to his table. The walk to the table where Stefon was sitting seemed like an eternity. Patty could feel the eyes on her and she was too afraid to look in any direction but straight ahead. When Patty finally reached the table, she placed her lunch tray down and took a seat.

"Hi Patty, did you find your classes okay?" Stefon asked as he reached for his hamburger.

"Yes I did, thanks to you. I owe you big time," Patty said as she opened her fruit punch and took a sip.

"Well, hello Patty, my name is Deion. I'm Stefon's best friend or so I think," Deion said extending his hand to Patty.

"It's nice to meet you, Deion," Patty said as she shook his hand.

"Sorry man, I wasn't thinking," Stefon said looking over at Patty.

After lunch, Deion had to rush off to class, leaving Stefon and Patty behind. Both Patty and Stefon signed up to take a volleyball class. When he found out that they were in the same class, Stefon was thrilled. Before class, the two stood outside the gym talking. "Patty, did you really mean it when you said you owe me?" Stefon asked glancing into Patty's eyes.

"Of course I meant it. You have been the only person besides Deion and the teachers that have spoken to me the entire day," Patty said, feeling somewhat sad because none of the girls were talking to her.

"Well, the school is having the annual back to school dance, would you do me the honor of being my date," Stefon asked.

"I would be honored to be your date, Stefon," Patty said, slightly blushing. The bell rang and a rush of students hurried past Patty and Stefon into the gym and they followed behind. Coach Smith was teaching the volleyball class. When Coach Smith saw Stefon, he was shocked to see how much Stefon had grown.

"Stefon Maynard is that you?" Coach Smith asked rubbing his eyes in amazement.

"Yeah Coach, it's me," Stefon said with a big grin on his face.

"So are you going out for football this year?" Coach asked.

"Yeah, I plan to," Stefon said.

"Well, I'll see you on the field, son," Coach said patting Stefon on the back.

The other students were coming out of the locker room when Stefon was on his way into the locker room. Everyone was sitting on the bleachers listening to Coach Smith when he came running out of the locker room tucking his tee shirt into his shorts. Stefon saw Patty sitting towards the end of the bleachers all alone so he went to sit next to her. All of the girls but one started pointing and whispering when Stefon sat by Patty. After Coach Smith went over the rules of the game, he divided the students into two even teams and told them to get a game started. Stefon, Patty and Mary, the one girl that wasn't pointing, all ended up on the same team. Mary approached Stefon and Patty and introduced herself to Patty. Mary stood about 5'0" tall, weighed 105 pounds. Everyone in the school called her light, bright, and damn near white because she was the lightest black in the school. The other girls would have nothing to do with her. They were jealous of her because she had long light brown hair, gray eyes and all of the boys were infatuated with her.

"Hello, my name is Mary," she said as she stood in front of Patty and Stefon.

"Nice to meet you, Mary. I'm Patty," Patty said giving Mary a big smile.

"Hey Mary, how's it going?" Stefon said, happy to see that a girl was now speaking to Patty. The three of them had a good time playing volleyball although the other girls avoided hitting the ball to Patty and Mary. By the end of the day, Stefon thought

Wrong Perception

he was in love with Patty. Before going home, Stefon asked Patty for her telephone number. She told him that she would have to ask her parents if she could give him the number.

The next day, Patty saw Stefon sitting on the top step leading into school, reading a book. She walked up and stood in front of him. He had to put his hand up like he was saluting in order to block the sun so that he could see who was standing in front of him.

"Good morning, Stefon," Patty said as she moved and sat beside him.

"Good morning, Patty. Glad to see that Turner High didn't drive you off," he said with a slight smile.

"No, they have to do more than ignore me. I'm here for an education, not to kiss people's behinds," Patty said with a serious look on her face.

"Well, I'm glad to see ya," Stefon said.

"I have something for you," Patty said as she went in her purse and pulled out a sheet of paper and gave it to Stefon. He couldn't tell what was written on the paper because it was folded. The way Stefon opened the paper you would have thought it was a present on Christmas morning. When he finally got the paper opened there were seven numbers on it—596-7120.

"My parents said that it was okay for me to give you our home number," Patty said.

"Good. Now I can call and ask your father about taking you to the dance Friday night," Stefon said putting the telephone number in his wallet.

"I see that you were studying your Algebra book," Patty said, changing the subject.

"Yeah, I'm not good at math and if I don't get a head start now, I won't be able to try out for the football team," Stefon said while opening the book.

"Well, if you need any help studying, feel free to ask me for help. I am very good at math," Patty said getting her book out of her backpack.

"Believe me, you're going to regret offering to help me," Stefon said, laughing. Just then, the busses started to pull into the loading zones. Stefon stood up and extended his hand to Patty in order to help her to her feet. They both grabbed their books and were off to homeroom. Deion joined them and the three talked and laughed all the way down the hallway. Before they reached homeroom, a girl named Sheila Thomas came out of nowhere and stood in front of them. Sheila was a chocolate beauty that stood 5'7" and weighed 110 pounds. Sheila was the captain of the junior varsity cheerleading squad and only dated football players. When she found out that Stefon was going out for the football team, she thought that she would date him, since she had already gone through the other players. Sheila had a Coke bottle figure that mesmerized most of the male students.

"Good morning, Stefon," Sheila said rolling her eyes at Patty.

"Good morning, Miss Rude, what can I do for you?" Stefon said in a sharp tone.

"I just wanted to know if you would be my date for the dance Friday night," Sheila said staring deep into Stefon's eyes.

"Sorry Sheila, but I already have a date for the dance," Stefon said moving closer to Patty.

"You're turning me down? That's a big mistake," Sheila said getting louder with every word.

"Look Sheila, it's nothing personal, but I'm dating someone," Stefon said now reaching over to hold Patty's hand.

"Your loss!" Sheila said storming down the hallway.

Patty started to swell with pride at the thought of being Stefon's girlfriend.

"Nice girl," Patty said sarcastically.

"Yeah, a little too nice for me," Stefon said.

"Are you sure you don't want to take her to the dance?" Patty asked.

"She's not my type," Stefon said squeezing Patty's hand.

"And who is your type?" Patty asked, now fishing for a name and hoping it would be hers.

"You are," Stefon said, now standing in front of Patty. Stefon leaned towards Patty and softly kissed her on the cheek and whispered in her ear, "Be my better half," in his sexiest voice. The warmth of his breath and tone of his voice caused chills to go through her body.

"It would be an honor to complete you," Patty said now blushing.

Wrong Perception

The bell rang for homeroom and the two ran down the hallway hand and hand to Mr. Bailey's class. They stepped inside the class just as the bell stopped. They laughed as they took their seats.

"Would the two of you like to let the rest of the class in on the joke? You know I love a good laugh," Mr. Bailey said taking a seat on top of his desk.

"No sir," Stefon said.

Just as Mr. Bailey was about to speak, the principal came over the intercom with the morning announcements.

"Good morning faculty and students of Turner High, today is Wednesday, August 27. I know all of you are happy to be back in school, and I wish all of you the best this school year."

Patty and Stefon appeared to be the ideal couple. Both of them were extremely attractive, and they complimented each other very well. As their junior year progressed, they appeared to be so in love. Stefon was the starting wide receiver on the football team, and Patty was helping him with his schoolwork. During their senior year, the two were deciding what college to attend after high school.

"I don't want to go to college far away from home."

"I don't either, Patty. Where do you want to go?"

"I was thinking about Southern University in Baton Rouge."

"Maybe I can get a football scholarship there, and we can go to college together."

The two agreed that they would both attend Southern University in Baton Rouge when they graduated from high school. Patty graduated with honors and accepted an academic scholarship, while Stefon accepted a football scholarship. When the couple arrived at Southern University, both of them worked hard at completing their degrees in three years by going to college year-round.

"We are doing it, baby. We have been going to school for two years now, and we have completed three years of classes. If we keep going to school year-round, we will finish next year," Patty said.

"Yeah, but it's been hard work. I am tired of going to school," Stefon said.

Patty completed her degree in Business Administration and Stefon completed his degree in Psychology. After Patty and Stefon graduated in June of 1962, they married and moved to Atlanta. Patty got a job working in the management division at Rich's department store, and Stefon landed a job working at the Atlanta Housing Authority. The couple bought a beautiful house on the southwest side of Atlanta, and planned to start a family. In May of 1963, Patty gave birth to their first child, a daughter that they named Monique. Five years later on March 5, 1967 Patty gave birth to their second child, a little boy named Reginald. Stefon became bored with the usual routine of coming home after work and sitting in front of the television. He began hanging out all night with some of his coworkers and began drinking heavily.

"Where have you been all night, Stefon? I have been waiting for you," Patty asked.

"I was out with the guys, just hanging out."

"You smell like you have been drinking, and it's three o'clock in the morning. The kids and I need you home. Reginald is a year old now, and he needs his father."

"I don't have time for this shit. I take good care of you and the kids, and I resent the fact that you would suggest that I don't take care of things around here."

"Stefon, you have been out the last three nights, and you have been drunk when you come home. You need to stop drinking and hanging out and spend more time with your family."

"Yeah, yeah, whatever. I'm going to bed. Goodnight."

Stefon started hanging out all night in bars, coming home as drunk as a skunk. Patty did everything she could to help Stefon to stop drinking, but nothing worked. After a year of trying to help her husband, Patty filed for divorce. Stefon agreed to give Patty the house and full custody of the kids in the divorce settlement. After a year and a half of being single, Patty remarried. Patty married a gentleman who was the director of operations at a local department store. Stefon, who was now receiving help for his alcohol addiction, was now the director of one of the housing developments, and he too, had remarried. With the $600 a month child support that Stefon was sending,

Wrong Perception

and the money that Patty and her new husband Ronald were making, Patty and her children had more than enough money to take care of things. The family was so wealthy that they had two new cars, bought a new home, and had an additional refrigerator for all of the superfluous food that they kept in their house.

4

Ronella and Byron

Ronella Mathews was born in Bulloch County, Georgia on March 25, 1945. She grew up on a farm in Bulloch County. She had three older brothers and one older sister. Being the baby in the family, Ronella was accustomed to attention from her siblings and other relatives. At the age of five, Ronella appeared to be the most outspoken child among the others in the neighborhood of the same age. By the time she reached her teens, she developed a good work ethic, which was to complete whatever she started. Her father use to brag to others in the neighborhood that she could pick cotton faster than anyone in Bulloch County. She was an excellent student in high school who loved English and literature. At James William High, where Ronella attended, the curriculum was geared towards earning a trade rather than preparing students to enter a college or university. Having worked on the farm all of her young life, Ronella was excited about the opportunity to graduate from high school and move to a big city where she could explore her horizons. When Ronella graduated from high school, she moved to New York City to attend a business college to learn general management skills. As a part-time job, she worked for a 75-year-old white woman as a maid and tutor to the woman's six-year-old grandson who lived with her. In her second year of school, she met a young man by the name of Byron German. Byron was a student at the business school, majoring in accounting.

"Hello, pretty lady, my name is Byron German. What is your name?" he asked.

"My name is Ronella."

"So tell me, pretty lady, where are you from?"

"Oh, from a small town in Georgia. Statesboro," Ronella responded.

"Oh yeah, I'm from the South myself." Byron said.

"What a small world, I thought you were from up north somewhere," Ronella said.

"No, I'm a good old country boy."

"Well, good old country boy, what brings you to New York?"

"I would say opportunity. You see, it's hard for a black man to attend college in the South, so I came here to spread my wings a little bit. You know what I mean?"

"I know exactly what you mean, that's why I'm here. Granted, it's not as hard for a black woman as it is for a black man, but it's still hard for all people of color."

"Ronella, I know this might sound awful forward, but do you have a boyfriend?"

"No, and I'm not looking for one either."

"Oh, I'm sorry, I didn't mean to make you mad." Byron said as he turned and started to walk away.

"Byron, wait a minute. I'm sorry, I shouldn't have been so rude. Would you like to get something to eat?"

"Okay, do you want to go to the sandwich shop across the street?" he asked.

"That's fine with me."

The owners of the sandwich shop were Muslims, members of the Nation of Islam. Byron ordered a fish sandwich as he always did and Ronella ordered the same.

"Ronella, where exactly is Bulloch County, and what kind of name is Ronella?"

"Statesboro, Georgia, if you must know," Ronella said, trying hard not to disclose the fact that she was very excited to meet someone from back home.

"Where are you from exactly?" Ronella inquired. At that point, she was at the edge of her seat. She thought to herself, *Could this be some kind of fate or coincidence?* Ronella never was big on coincidence. She bought into the idea that everyone was captain of his or her circumstances.

When Byron answered that he was from South Carolina, Ronella seemed disappointed. She wanted the answer to be

Wrong Perception

Georgia. New York is so fast and the men even faster. Ronella felt quite uncomfortable with fast living and the fast people of the big city.

Finally, she thought, *I have met someone from home, someone from my comfort zone. So what if South Carolina wasn't Georgia, it was close enough.*

Byron did not know it, but he scored many points with Ronella. She was all smiles inside, but nonchalant on the outside. When they finished their sandwiches, there was an awkward lull in the conversation. Both wanted to continue the conversation, and both tried to think of the perfect thing to say. They were equally intimidated by each other. They did manage, however, to set up the next date and exchange phone numbers. The courtship was well on its way. Ronella went back to the house she was working in. Her boss knew something was different about her. Ronella seemed happier, more comfortable. Byron's sister and brother-in-law recognized a difference in him as well. Byron was usually very introverted with infrequent emotional eruptions when the situation warranted any strong emotions. The issue of race and discrimination was an issue that would make Byron erupt like a volcano. Because of discrimination, Byron had to come to New York to work as a postal carrier. He would not be hired in the South for the same position. Although it was a federal job, the managers and supervisors down south were racists. Byron noticed after a few months of working on the job up North that two of the other black male employees were dating white women. This incensed him. Byron hated white men and vowed to never date, let alone marry, outside of his race. Byron usually delivered the mail, ate dinner at the local Muslim restaurant and went home. He pretty much kept to himself, not saying much to family when he would visit them, or people passing by on the street. After meeting Ronella, and dating her for a few months, he was now talking more to his relatives. Whatever had happened to Byron, his relatives were very happy, because now he was actually a pleasure to have around. The only time Byron was as happy was at dinnertime, especially if the main course was fried chicken. The family did not ask Byron what caused the difference in his disposition. Byron did not tell them either. It was not until his brother-in-law caught Byron writing a love letter to Ronella that he knew Byron was in love. Clinton read the letter.

> Dear Ronella,
> I have never been happier, than the day I meet you. You bring me joy and happiness in the midst of my sadness and disappointments. I love you more than life itself, and I will do whatever it takes to keep you by my side . . .

Clinton realized that although Byron was different these days, he was the same in many ways. Byron did not realize that Clinton was reading over his shoulder. When he did realize that he was not alone, he attempted to shield his letter with his hand. When he looked in Clinton's face, Byron knew that his brother-in-law must have read the letter. Byron began telling Clinton everything about Ronella. He got so excited talking about Ronella, that it seemed as if he was confessing something after holding it in for so long. Byron's sister wanted to know what the conversation was about, especially since it was Byron doing all the talking and this time it was not about race. This conversation was about love.

Byron and Ronella began to spend a lot of time together. They found comfort and warmth in each other that could not be found in a fast and uncomfortable city. They had a home in each other. Their love was young and impetuous, crazy, sexy, comfortable, cool and warm all at the same time. Together they felt strong and confident of who they were and where they were from. The intimacy was a power that they just knew no one else had. They wanted to be on, in and around each other all of the time.

After several mornings of stomach aches and nausea, Ronella saw a doctor and found out that she was pregnant. Things changed. Byron saw the world and the current times as so cold with few opportunities for black people. He did not want to have any kids.

"I love you Ronella. Maybe if things were different for blacks, I would want kids."

"Well, the baby will be here soon, so you better find a way to want children."

"I will, it's just going to take some time."

Wrong Perception

"Well, I hope nine months is long enough."

To Byron having kids born to him was like him coming into the cold world again. He hated the idea of having children and he hated Ronella for being pregnant. Byron and Ronella began finding it hard to make each other comfortable. Byron would start an argument about the most trivial things, which was a clear sign to Ronella that her having a baby was the real issue. Ronella suggested to Byron that they separate for a little while to see if things would get better. The two parted and promised each other that they would keep in touch after the baby was born.

Feeling that Ronella was no longer the love of his life and with the recent civil rights laws that were passed, there were now a few employment opportunities for blacks in the South. Byron decided to move back to South Carolina and seek employment. Ronella remained for a while and then moved back home to Statesboro. In June of 1963, Ronella gave birth to a little boy she named Victor. Determined not to remain at home, Ronella decided to move to Atlanta where employment opportunities for blacks were on the rise. When Ronella arrived in Atlanta, she applied for several jobs and finally found one as a receptionist in a doctor's office. She was determined that she wanted to be more than a receptionist, so she spent her evenings studying for the real estate agent exam. After five weeks of preparation, she passed the real estate exam. Meanwhile, back in South Carolina, Byron was feeling like something or someone was missing from his life. One day while talking to his sister, she asked Byron if he knew how Ronella and the baby were doing. Tears came to Byron's eyes because it wasn't until now that he realized what was missing from his life. As soon as Byron hung up the telephone with his sister, he started thinking about whatever became of his lost love and his son. He remembered that Ronella had moved back to Statesboro because she needed the support of her family during and after the birth of their child. Byron tore his apartment up looking for his old address book because he wanted to find his son so he could be a real father, unlike his father. He finally found the book in a shoe box of important papers on the top shelf of his closet. Byron fumbled as he tried to find Ronella's mother's telephone number. He located the phone number and quickly dialed before he lost his nerve.

"Hello?" the voice on the line said.

"Hello, is this the Mathews' residence?" Byron asked.

"Yes it is, what can I do for ya?" the old country voice asked.

"Is Ms. Ronella Mathews there, I'm an old friend of hers," Byron said hoping the person wouldn't ask him who he was, because he knew Ronella probably badmouthed him to her family.

"Well, you must not have been in touch with her for a while sonny," the old man said.

"No, I haven't, is she all right?" Byron asked with concern in his voice.

"Oh, she's fine. I didn't mean to scare you, but she and the baby are now living in Atlanta."

"Is there any way I could get her telephone number and address in Atlanta? I would love to surprise her," Byron said now reaching for a pen and something to write on.

"Where did you say you knew my baby Ronella from?" the old man asked.

"I am a friend of hers from New York," Byron said hoping that this was enough information for the old man.

"Well, I guess it's all right to give you my baby's number and address, hold on while I get the info," the old man said dropping the phone on the table.

Byron waited patiently for him to return to the telephone.

"Sonny, ya still there?" the old man asked.

"Yes, I'm still here," Byron said.

"Well, Ron's address is 14-A Cascade Road, Atlanta, Georgia 30303 and her number is 444-763-2587. Did ya get that?" the old man asked.

"Yes sir, I did, thank you very much. You don't know how happy you've made me," Byron said hanging up the telephone. Byron started dialing Ronella's telephone number, but then hung up before anyone answered. He felt he would rather surprise her and his son in person. Byron flipped through the telephone book and looked up the number to the bus station. He called and got the first bus leaving for Atlanta. He packed his bag and headed out the door. Byron had very little clothes in his bag and only $120 in his pocket, but he knew this was the right move to make.

Wrong Perception

Byron was one of twenty passengers that were on the bus. He sat close to the back in a window seat. As the bus started to leave the station, Byron stared out the window. He couldn't help but think about his reunion with Ronella and his son Victor. The bus ride seemed like an eternity.

Everything seemed to be getting better for Ronella until she received a surprise visit from Byron four years after his departure. When Byron popped up at her apartment, Ronella had mixed emotions. She was happy to see the only man that she had ever loved, but was still mad at him for leaving her and not helping to raise their child.

"Hi Ronella. I know that you are not very happy to see me, but I have a lot to talk to you about. Can I come in?" Byron asked.

"I guess so, come on in."

"Where is my boy?"

"He is in his room playing. Wait in the living room until I get him."

As Ronella entered Victor's room, she said, "Victor, someone's here to see you."

"Who is it, Mom?"

"It's your father. Come out here so you can meet him."

"Okay Mom," Victor responded.

"Here he is," Ronella said as Victor entered the living room.

"Come over here and give your father a hug," Byron said.

"Mom, is he really my daddy?"

"Yes he is son, go give your dad a hug."

After Victor hugged Byron, Ronella said, "Victor, you can go back to your room and play now, your father and I have a lot to talk about."

After Victor was out of the room Ronella asked, "Well Byron, what brings you here?"

"I have realized that I made a terrible mistake by leaving you and little Victor. I want a second chance to be the father that my boy needs. If you give me a second chance, I will never disappoint you again."

"You know what, Byron?"

"What's that, baby?"

"I have been mad as hell at you the last four years. I must admit though, I still love you," Ronella said as she punched Byron in the chest.

"I'm sorry baby. I know what I did was not something any man can be proud of, but please, baby, give me a chance to show you that I have learned from my mistake."

"You have to prove yourself all over again. I'm willing to work on this relationship for our son," Ronella said.

"Thanks baby, you don't know what this opportunity means to me. I really am sorry," Byron said as he began kissing Ronella on the cheek and caressing her hands.

It was like old times between the two of them. Byron picked Ronella up and carried her to the bedroom. Ronella was hesitant at first, but after a couple of hours, Ronella ripped Byron's blue button-down shirt open, popping off every button.

"Hurry and take off your pants," Ronella said.

"I'm hurrying as fast as I can," Byron said excitedly.

Since it was about eight o'clock at night, Ronella was only wearing a nightgown. She pulled off her nightgown and began helping Byron take off his shoes and jeans. "I have missed you Byron, make love to me," Ronella said.

The two made passionate love like there was no tomorrow. After the lovemaking episode, the couple discussed a possible marriage in the future. Byron moved in with Ronella and promised to help raise their son Victor. A couple of weeks later, Byron was able to find a job at a post office in Atlanta as a mail carrier. Ronella found out that she was pregnant and expecting their second child. During the first three months of Ronella's pregnancy, Byron and Ronella began to argue about everything. One day Byron got so fed up with the arguments that he decided to go to a local tavern to get a drink.

"I can't take any more of this arguing, I'm going down to the tavern and have myself a drink," Byron said.

"Well, you just do that, I don't care."

"I'll see you later, Ronella."

"Yeah, whatever," Ronella responded.

Wrong Perception

When Byron got down to the tavern, he was singing the blues to one of the locals who was also down on his luck. "My name is Byron, what's yours?"

"My name is Calvin Jules, pull up a seat, my friend. What brings you here?"

"Me and my girlfriend got into a fight. How about you, what brings you here?"

"I'm so tired of my old lady, but I'm staying for the kids. My youngest will be eighteen next year, and I'm leaving the bitch."

Just as Calvin finished his sentence, Yolanda Parker entered the tavern. Immediately she had eyes for Byron. "Byron, did you see the way that lady was looking at you?"

"No. What lady?"

"That pretty brown skin lady, with the long black hair, wearing the white and black dress." Byron turned around and looked directly at Ms. Parker. Ms. Parker smiled and waved at Byron and he waved back.

"You know the funny thing about all of this, Calvin?"

"No, what's that man?"

"When one black woman makes you feel like shit, there is always another that makes you feel good again. Black men don't want to fuck around on their ladies, it's just that when the white man beats you down all day, and the white women roll their eyes at you, somebody has got to lift your spirits to make you feel like a man again. I have been called 'boy' and 'nigger' so much that sometimes I forget my name is Byron. Black women don't endure the same pain as black men, because both black and white men seek black women. The only person who cares about the black man outside of his family is another black woman. Black women love us, man. When they look us up and down and smile, like that pretty lady has just done to me, I feel good about myself."

"You don't need no woman to make ya feel good, man. You should be able to make yourself feel good."

"Yeah, you're right but the Nation of Islam teaches me that the white man is the devil. The white man took this land from the Indians and has either enslaved or discriminated against us for the last four hundred years. White men will do whatever they can to keep us blacks down. I want to feel good about myself, but getting a second class education, having 'colored only' bathrooms and restaurants and living in a substandard house doesn't make me feel too good. Can you believe that the devils are still saying that blacks are inferior to whites? They have not allowed us to get a quality education, yet the racist bastards say that we are intellectually inferior. Go figure."

"Yeah, you're right, the white man is no doubt the devil," Calvin said.

"That's why I say we need our black women to continue to lift a brother up."

"Yo, man, she's coming over here," Calvin said as the two turned to look directly at Yolanda as she approached their table.

"Hi fellows, my name is Yolanda Parker. How are you guys doing?"

"Were doing pretty good. Would you like to sit down?" Calvin asked.

"Yes, thanks for the invitation," Yolanda said as she sat down and looked directly at Byron. "So tell me, what is your name, handsome?"

"My name is Byron German and this is Calvin Jules."

"It's nice to meet you Mr. Jules, but I want to know if your friend here, Mr. German, is married?"

"No, but I do have a girlfriend," Byron answered.

"Well, I don't want to take you from your girlfriend, I just want to spend some time with you," Yolanda said.

"That's awful generous of you," Byron said.

"You are just so cute. I will give you my phone number and whenever you want to call or spend time with me, just give me a call," Yolanda said.

"Thanks Yolanda, I just might take you up on your offer."

One day, Ronella got out of bed, took her shower and got dressed to head to the office. She told Byron that she was going to drop Victor off at the day care center and that she would be showing houses to clients.

"Byron, I'll see you later, baby. I have to meet with a client at eleven o'clock."

"All right Ronella, I'll be working late today. Could you cook dinner when you come home?"

"No! Make it your damn self," Ronella said.

Wrong Perception

"Now what's wrong?" Byron asked.

"Nothing's wrong. I've got to get out of here," Ronella said.

When Ronella arrived at the real estate office at 9 A.M., there was a note on her desk. The note read, *Your eleven o'clock appointment has called in and cancelled.* Ronella did not have another appointment until 3 P.M., so she thought that it would be a good time to go home and make up with Byron. She knew that she had been rude to him and she wanted to apologize. Byron did not have to be at work until one o'clock. When Ronella got home, she noticed an unfamiliar car in the driveway. When she put her key in the door, she noticed that the door was already open. When she entered the house, she heard the stereo blasting and a woman's voice coming from the bedroom. When Ronella made her way to the bedroom, she found Byron in bed with Yolanda Parker. Being the strong woman that she was, Ronella turned and walked away unseen by Byron or Yolanda. When Ronella got back to her office, she cried her eyes out.

"What's wrong, Ronella?" Peter Wilson, one of her coworkers, asked.

"It's my boyfriend. I went home to surprise him for lunch, because my eleven o'clock appointment cancelled, and I found him in the bed with another woman. He didn't see me, so I got back in the car and came back to work."

"Oh Ronella, I know it must be devastating, but you're a strong woman. You will make it through this. We are here for you if you need anything."

"Thanks Pete, I really appreciate your support."

Ronella couldn't believe that she gave Byron another chance to hurt her a second time. Several of the other real estate agents tried to console her, but she cried frantically for hours. After work, she picked up Victor from the day care and returned home later that evening. Byron was not home when Ronella pulled into the driveway. Byron returned several hours later to find his clothes outside on the front lawn with a note attached that read, *I hope that slut you're fucking is going to help you pay child support, you lying motherfucker.* Byron stood outside of the apartment trying to apologize.

"Ronella, she didn't mean anything to me. It's over baby, I promise. I'll never see her again."

"If she did not mean anything to you, you would not have been in my house with her."

Ronella vowed that she would never take Byron back again. On April 16, 1967, Ronella gave birth to her second son, Stacy.

5

The Start of a Beautiful Friendship

The year was 1973. Many of the black families in Atlanta heard about the new opportunity to bus their children to the best public school in Atlanta, Barton Chapel Elementary. Carolyn Jones, Patty Maynard, and Ronella Mathews were able to enroll their children.

It was fall and James Jones, Reginald Maynard and Stacy Mathews were now six years old and headed to first grade at Barton Chapel Elementary School. When they arrived at school, the boys noticed that they were the only three blacks in the class and felt a sense of familiarity with each other. The boys introduced themselves.

"My name is James Jones and I have two brothers Johnny and Jeff and one sister named Gina."

"My name is Reginald Maynard and I have an older sister named Monique."

"My name is Stacy Mathews and I have an older brother named Victor."

The three boys hit it off instantly. All three lived on the south side of Atlanta, but the school was on the north side. Barton Chapel was located near the more financially affluent, that was why the school was considered the best elementary school in the Atlanta public school system.

As the next few years progressed, the young boys became inseparable. The boys would sit next to each other during class and would eat together at lunch. During the summers, the boys would call each other on the telephone and visit each other's homes.

Things started to get worse for the Jones family. With the frustration of the move and the divorce, James and Johnny seemed to become the scapegoats for all of Carolyn's physical and emotional indignity. It appeared to always be a power struggle between them.

Now being a single parent, Carolyn became very austere. She would normally beat the boys for the most trivial justifications and in turn the two would try to attain some type of control by taking it out on their younger brother Jeff or anyone else that crossed them. Therefore, the regular beatings at home led to trouble at school. Johnny was an outstanding student so he did not receive as many beatings as James did. James did poorly in school and would constantly start fights with his classmates. Consequently from the fights, James was suspended from school.

Carolyn would whip James whenever one of his teachers would call, or whenever Jeff told his mother that James fought with him. She would whip James so bad sometimes that she would draw blood. She would whip him with extension cords, broom handles, leather belts or anything else she could get her hands on. Once while standing outside, she picked up a brick and threw it at James, tearing the skin off his arm. She would always make James strip down to his underwear, so that whatever she was whipping him with would hit against his skin. She wanted to be assured that he would feel the agonizing pain. On several occasions when James would get suspended from school, Carolyn would batter him so badly with an electrical extension cord, that you would have sworn that he must have tried to run away from a slave master. James would have numerous lacerations transversely on his back and legs. Whenever James' teacher would call his home, he would endeavor to run from his mother, but she would always run him down and beat him.

"I am so tired of you! You are just like your father," she would often tell James while beating him.

"But Mama, I was not trying to do anything wrong. It was a mistake."

"Shut up, boy, you always do everything wrong on purpose, so stop telling me it was a goddamn mistake," Carolyn would say, as she would hit James at least thirty to forty times with a belt or an extension cord.

Wrong Perception

The clothes and shoes that James and his siblings wore were usually purchased at irregular clothing shops and purchased for half the normal price. James's clothes and shoes were so cheap that the other students made jokes about his clothes almost daily. James would often ask Reginald or Stacy if he could sport some of their clothes. "Hey, James, do all of your clothes look that bad?" the students would say and laugh in unison.

James and Reginald lived in the same neighborhood, so they would spend time together after school customarily playing basketball at Reginald's house. After playing basketball, the boys would usually go to Reginald's room, listen to the music on the radio and talk about what they planned to do the following day.

"So what are we going to do tomorrow?" James asked.

"Oh, I don't know, what's on your mind, buddy boy?"

"I thought you might want to go with me and sign up for the Little League basketball team at Adams Park?"

"Yeah, I'll go."

"Well, I think we need to be there by 5:30 to sign up."

"Okay, let me go and ask my mother. She will probably take us."

"Hey, Mom, James wants to know if I can play Little League basketball at Adams Park."

"How much does it cost to play, baby?"

"Hey James! How much does it cost?" Reginald yelled to James who was in the next room.

"It cost twenty-five dollars."

"Did you hear him, Mom?"

"Yes, I heard him, baby."

"Well, can I play Mom, please?"

"Sure baby, if it's what you really want to do."

"Thanks, Mom."

James and Reginald immediately called Stacy and asked him if he wanted to play. Stacy told his friends that he wasn't interested. Stacy was a mama's boy that enjoyed staying home and watching television.

Reginald and James really enjoyed playing on the same basketball team. The experience brought them even closer as friends. The two were able to lead their team to become Little League champions.

Monique really didn't care too much for James because she knew that he came from a poor family. She often wondered what her brother saw in him. James's family was now going without food on a regular basis. James hated going home because there was infrequently any food and he and his brothers fought constantly.

James would go to Reginald's house for two reasons: the first, to play, and the second, to consume a meal. Monique would always find a way to insult James whenever he showed up at her house.

"What are you doing over here?" Monique would ask.

"I just came to play with Reginald."

"You are always over here. Do you have any other friends?"

"I have a couple of other friends, but I really enjoy coming over here."

"Well, I wish you wouldn't come over here so much."

"Why is that?"

"Because I don't like you. You always come over here eating up our food. What's the problem little ugly boy, you don't have any food at your house?"

"Oh leave him alone Monique, he didn't do anything to you," Reginald would say.

"I'm just tired of him coming over here eating up our food."

"Don't worry about her, man. She always says the same stupid stuff when you come over here. My mother doesn't mind that you eat over here, so don't worry about her."

James was infatuated with Monique. She was beautiful, athletic and had a body that wouldn't quit. She was the starting point guard on her high school basketball team and played centerfield on the softball team. James was infatuated with her just as many young boys were, and it hurt him deeply when she insulted him.

Reginald was a very good-looking kid. He looked like a young Reverend Jesse Jackson. Even as early as elementary school, the girls thought that Reginald was the cutest boy in school. So many girls would call his house, that his mother would tell him that he needed to pick one and tell the others to stop calling.

Wrong Perception

"Baby, you need to stop giving out our phone number. I'm tired of hearing that phone ring so much."

"Mama, I'm not giving my number out, I don't know where the girls are getting it from."

Stacy was the unobtrusive one of the three, but was also well groomed like Reginald. Stacy was mediocre looking, but had a quiet demeanor. The young girls were very fond of him. His skin tone was brown and like Reginald, he wore nice accouterments and shoes.

By the third grade, James would sometimes beat up the other kids so crudely that their parents would get involved, threatening to seriously hurt him if he continued to beat up their kids. Normally, James would be suspended for three days for his behavior, and his mother would have to take him back to school and have a conference with the principal. James was suspended four times in the third grade. This deportment continued through the fourth grade.

When James was in the fifth grade, he practically fell in love with his teacher, Mrs. Pariah. James thought that Mrs. Pariah was the prettiest teacher in the school. She was always well-dressed and wore a perfume that James was crazy about. James would normally sit in the back of the class, but in Mrs. Pariah's class James would sit in the front row. Mrs. Pariah would normally give the students in her class a hug before class, and James looked forward to that hug everyday.

After listening to the gossip from other teachers in the school, Mrs. Pariah took James on as her special project because she appeared to be the only teacher that he gave his undivided attention to. James did not fight as much as he did the previous two years, but he was still stigmatized as the class bully. Reginald and Stacy continued to be James's friend although he would start fights with them, too.

James did not do well on standardized tests. After failing to score at the fifth grade level on the California Achievement Test, he was labeled learning-disabled and put into special education classes. Once James's father got word that James was not as adroit as his other children, he started showing favoritism toward Gina, Johnny and Jeff, who were considered to be healthy, glistening children.

"So tell me, Jeff and Johnny, how many A's did you make this quarter?"

"I made all A's again, Daddy," Jeff said.

"How many A's is that?"

"Six."

"How about you, Johnny?"

"I made five A's and one B daddy." Johnny said.

"Well I am going to give you twenty dollars for every A."

"How about you Gina, how did you do?"

"I made three A's, two B's, and one C."

"How about you James, how many A's did you make?"

"I made all C's, Daddy."

"Well, anyway, Jeff here's one hundred and twenty dollars, Johnny this is one hundred dollars for you, and Gina here's your sixty dollars."

For the next few years, James continued to improve on his ability to play baseball, while causing havoc in the classrooms.

Reginald continued to gain popularity from the other students, while maintaining a solid B+ average. During football season, James would go to Reginald's football games on Saturday morning to watch him play.

"Mrs. Maynard, this is James calling. I was wondering if you could pick me up so that I could go and watch Reginald play?"

"Sure, James, I'll pick you up in a few minutes. Have you eaten yet?"

"No, ma'am."

"Okay, I'll bring you something to eat."

"Thanks, Mrs. Maynard."

Reginald was so good at football that he made the other players appear to be a lot younger than he was. Reginald was so good that he would score a touchdown almost every time he touched the football. Furthermore, all of the young cheerleaders on the sideline would talk about how attractive he was and how well he played football.

"Reginald Maynard is my boyfriend," one of the cheerleaders would say.

"I don't think so, girl, he is my boyfriend," another cheerleader would say while the other cheerleaders laughed.

Wrong Perception

Their favorite cheer was "Reginald, Reginald he's our man, if he can't do it nobody can."

In the winter season of James and Reginald's fifth grade year, they played basketball together on the same recreation team at Adams Park. They would either catch a bus to get to practice, or Reginald's mother would take them. Reginald did not care too much for baseball, but in the spring he would go to Adams Park to watch James play.

During the summer after James's fifth grade year at Barton Chapel, Carolyn finally allowed James and his siblings to live with their father for the summer. Ironically, although James was well provided for while living with his father, he was picked up for shoplifting in a Zayre Department store. James thought that his father would be furious with him. Once he got home, after his stepmother Laverne picked him up from the store his father asked, "What were you thinking about young man?"

"I saw some toys that I thought my younger half sisters would enjoy playing with. They are called finger pops. When you squeeze one of them between your thumb and another finger, they pop up in the air."

"Why didn't you buy them, son?"

"I didn't have any money, and I thought Dharma and Laura would enjoy playing with them."

"Well, I understand that you are sorry for what you did, because I can see it on your face and hear it in your voice. I want you to go to your room and think about what you did."

James was stunned that Michael did not whip him. Carolyn had painted this picture of a monster, and James was surprised that Michael just told him to go to his room and think about what he did rather than whip him. At the end of the summer, James and his siblings moved back in with Carolyn.

6

Middle School Years

In 1979, Reginald, James and Stacy entered Sego Middle School. Sego was three times the size of Barton Chapel. The darker complexion blacks would harass James because he was light skinned. Reginald and Stacy made friends with the bullies on the first day of school, so they did not get harassed.

"What are you looking at you high yellow punk?" Maurice asked.

"I'm not looking at anything, I'm just trying to go to class." James replied.

"Oh, yeah, well take this kick up the ass with you," the other students would say.

"Why don't you guys leave me alone, I haven't done anything to you."

"Fuck you, pretty boy."

"Yeah, whatever," James would say as the boys would punch or kick him.

This unfortunate racial confrontation occurred almost daily for James during his sixth and seventh grade years. He would tell his mother about the episodes, but his mother refused to believe that things could really be that bad.

James was frustrated because there were no other students in his class that would help him fight the guys. He was so angry that he continued his devilish ways by starting fights with other students in the school. James would slap another kid for merely looking at him the wrong way. If someone were to say something to James that he did not like, he would punch them until he got tired, just as his mother did to him when he got a beating. James was suspended practically every other week. After every suspension, James's mother would whip him until most of his body was red and bruised and would try to convince him that she really loved him.

"James, I will whip you every time you get into trouble. If I don't whip you now, the world is going to whip your ass later. All you complain about is what your friends have. None of them have any substance, their parents give them everything they want. You on the other hand, have learned to work for and appreciate everything you have. When these young friends of yours get older, they won't have the desire that you will have to put in an honest day's work, just wait and see what I tell you," Carolyn said.

After failing to score the required minimum score on the California Achievement Test that was given at Sego, James was assigned to the learning disabled department in the school. His daily assignments included basic math, reading and taking a spelling test. James was not as intimidating anymore because many of the students began to have their growth spurts, while he appeared to be the same size in the sixth grade that he was in the fifth. Many of the students were now seeking revenge because they were now bigger than James was. James was suspended from school for fighting ten times between sixth and seventh grades.

By the eighth grade, after the first quarter of school, James was unable to test out of the learning disabled program and was enrolled for another term.

Stacy decided that he did not want to tryout for the football team, but Reginald and James tried out. On the Monday morning following the week of tryouts, both Reginald and James found out that they made the team.

"Hey, man, we made it," James said.

"Oh, I knew we would, the coach kind of hinted towards it last week." Reginald said.

"Well, that's good, why didn't you tell me?"

"I wasn't sure, so I didn't say anything."

"Well, anyway, we made it. Congratulations, Reginald."

"Yeah congratulations, buddy."

When Reginald got home and told his mother that he had made the football team, she was very happy.

Wrong Perception

"I'm so proud of you, son. I wanted to do so much when I was in school, but couldn't afford it. That's why I make sure you don't want for anything. I keep plenty of food in the refrigerator, beautiful clothes on your back and give you money whenever you need it, baby, I love you and Monique very much."

"I love you, too, Mama."

Reginald was obviously a better football player than James and the other players that tried out, and his experience was evident during the season. James was not a starter but played quite a bit during each game. Reginald was the star running back on offense and the starting safety on defense. Reginald scored a touchdown in every game. He led his team in tackles and touchdowns. At the end of the season, Reginald was recognized as the most valuable player.

James had the hots for a young lady named Shayna Butler. James thought that she was one of the prettiest girls in the eighth grade. Shayna would often talk to James in the cafeteria, but when another student would ask Shayna if she liked James, she would always deny it. One day, James got very upset when Shayna denied having feelings for him.

"What's wrong, James?" Shayna asked.

"I know you like me, and I can't understand why you can't admit it." James said.

"How do you know whether I like you or not?"

"Well, I will say it like this, either be my girlfriend or don't ever speak to me again," James said as he turned and walked away.

"Okay, I will be your girlfriend," Shayna responded.

"What did you say?" James asked.

"You heard me right, I said that I will be your girlfriend," Shayna said as the school bell rang for the students to go back to class.

James could not believe what he had heard. Shayna was going to be his first girlfriend. James was so excited. He could not wait until the school day ended so that he could spend some time with his new girlfriend. After school, James walked up to Shayna and said "Hey, were you serious about what you said earlier?"

"I sure was. I really do like you. I am sorry that I made you feel bad trying to deny my feelings," Shayna said.

Why would you deny that you like someone?"

"Because your reputation is just so bad. I know my friends are going to have something to say about this. I don't care what they say, I like you James Jones."

"Can I have your phone number so I can call you?" James asked.

"Yes, let me write it on a piece of paper for you," Shayna replied. "James?"

"Yes, Shayna."

"Could you stop being so bad? You know, fighting all the time?" Shayna asked.

"I don't want you to break up with me. I am going to do my best," James said.

"Well, that's all I can ask from anyone."

James dated Shayna during the fall quarter. At the end of the fall quarter, Shayna was told by another student that they thought James's mother wore a wig.

Due to the divorce, Carolyn was literally pulling her hair out. She started wearing wigs almost daily. James, like any other student, was embarrassed when Shayna found out.

"James, someone told me that your mother wears a wig," Shayna said.

"Who in the world told you something stupid like that." James replied.

"I'm not going to say who told me, I just want to know if it's true," Shayna said. "Because if she does wear a wig, I think that is very funny."

"Well, she doesn't wear a wig, and if she did, I don't understand what's so fucking funny," James said, getting upset.

"Well, I see you are getting defensive, so it must be true," Shayna said.

"Fuck you, Shayna. Don't ever call me again," James said as he hung up the telephone.

Shayna tried to call James back, but he did not want to have anything to do with her. James and Shayna never spoke again.

In the winter, James and Reginald tried out for the basketball team and the two were selected to play. To the surprise of both of them, James was actually the better basketball player. During basketball season, James started the season as the starting point guard and co-captain. Reginald would play during the games, but he was not a starter. James was the team's best free throw shooter, so he would always shoot the technical fouls for the team. Nearing the end of the season, James's paternal grandmother died and he had to leave school to attend the funeral. During his absence, a player who remained the starting point guard the remainder of the season, replaced James at point guard. After basketball season, neither James nor Reginald tried out for the track team freeing up a lot of time for James and Reginald to hang out with Stacy.

During the spring, Sego sponsored a talent show. James thought that it would be a good idea if he, along with Reginald and two other students, performed a skating routine in the talent show. James knew that the talent show would be held in the gymnasium, and that he and his friends would probably win the competition if they were allowed to skate. Fortunately, the boys were allowed to skate and won first place in the talent show. That day was one of the happiest days of their lives. The young girls were congratulating them with hugs and kisses after the show. With only a few months left in school, James and Reginald would spend time with Stacy going to Six Flags, the movies, and the roller skating rink.

One day, all of the eighth grade students were told to report to the gym for an important information briefing. Representatives from the local high schools wanted to talk to the eighth grade students about their plans.

The representatives were there mainly to talk about what their high schools offered that the other ones did not. A representative from Brookview High School spoke to the students first, mentioning the fact that it was a school of performing arts and as a student you could learn to sing, dance, play an instrument, or act in the drama program. The representative went on to say that its sports program was unparalleled to any school in Atlanta because it not only offered the usual baseball, basketball and football, but the school was the only public school in Atlanta with a wrestling team. James was so impressed that Brookview had a wrestling team that he did not hang around in the auditorium to hear what the other representatives had to say about their schools. James' mind was made up. He was going to Brookview and was going to tryout for the wrestling team.

Reginald was informed that Brookview traditionally beat the other schools in football, so Brookview was also the school of his choice. Stacy decided that he did not want to part from his friends and decided that he too would attend Brookview.

All three boys graduated from Sego Middle School and continued to hang out at Six Flags and the skating rink during the summer.

7

Glory Days of High School

During the fall, James got a chance to meet with the wrestling coach to find out what he needed to do to make the team. Coach Daryl Alexander was the wrestling coach. He told James that he needed to buy some books on college freestyle wrestling, be in excellent physical condition and be ready for some stiff competition. James started working out with weights and running two miles a day. Wrestling season was not until the winter, so James had plenty of time to get in shape. James' brother Johnny and Reginald were preparing to tryout for the junior varsity football team. One day after school, Reginald was talking to Johnny, about trying out for the junior varsity football team.

"Hey, Johnny, why doesn't James tryout for the football team?" Reginald asked.

"Hell, I don't know, all he talks about is that stupid wrestling stuff."

"What is it, man, you don't like wrestling or something?"

"No, it's not that, James just can't seem to stop being full of himself. He always talks about how good he thinks he's going to be."

"Your brother always did like kicking people's ass, man. Who knows, he might be pretty good at it," Reginald said.

"I sure hope so, because he is sure getting on my nerves talking about it."

"So tell me, what position are you trying out for, Johnny?" Reginald asked.

"I don't know man, I just want to play football," Johnny replied. "How about you man?"

"I am going to tryout for running back."

"With all of your years of experience, you should do well at whatever position you play."

"I sure hope so," Reginald responded.

When Johnny returned home that evening, he started a conversation with James. "Hey, James, Reginald asked me why you didn't tryout for the football team."

"Oh, yeah, what did you tell him?"

"I told him that all you talk about is trying out for the wrestling team."

"You're damn right, I'm looking forward to kicking some ass on the wrestling mat."

"You haven't ever wrestled before, why do you think you're going to be so good?"

"Fuck you man! I know I'm going to be good. You just wait and see."

"Don't get all defensive, boy, I just asked a question. I was not trying to put you down. Hell you come from the same stock that I do, you should be good."

"My fault Johnny, I took it the wrong way and I apologize."

"You don't have to apologize, just be yourself, and you will do fine."

"I appreciate your support, man," James replied.

Johnny was a natural at football. During the season, Johnny played cornerback and led the team in tackles. Reginald led the team in touchdowns with eight. Johnny could play practically any position on the field, but he didn't care too much for the sport. After Johnny's junior varsity season playing football, he didn't play again. Johnny had grown up playing baseball and decided that he would devote all of his attention to it.

James, having lost so many fights in middle school, was determined that he would be an outstanding wrestler so he would be able to defend himself whenever the opportunity presented itself.

Reginald enjoyed playing basketball, but football was unquestionably his favorite sport. He was preparing to try out for the junior varsity basketball team, and was playing "pick-up" games every chance he could after school. Reginald would always tell James, "I will play basketball, but football is where my heart is."

It was finally the big day. Reginald tried out for the basketball team and James tried out for the wrestling team. A week later, both of the boys found out that they made their respective teams. On the bus ride home, the boys talked a little bit about everything, the past, the present, and their future plans. As the bus got closer to downtown Atlanta, James realized that he was getting hungry.

"Yo, man, can you loan me a couple of dollars when we get downtown so I can eat at McDonald's?" James asked.

"I don't know why you said loan, hell, your broke ass will never pay me back."

"I will pay you back, just loan me a couple of dollars?"

"All right, man, I was just kidding, how much money do you need?" Reginald asked.

"Two dollars, man, just enough to buy me a cheeseburger and some french fries."

"Here, man, but I know you can't pay me back. With your broke ass."

"Thanks, man, I will pay you back, don't worry about it," James responded.

Approximately three weeks later, James was participating in his first junior varsity wrestling match. He won the match by pinning his opponent in the first period. Johnny was on hand to watch his brother, and was the first to congratulate him after the match.

"You are pretty good at this, boy," Johnny told James. "You made your opponent look like a wimp out there."

"I am just happy that I won my first match and that you were here to see it," James replied.

Coach Alexander approached James. "James, that was a real good performance for your first match."

"Thanks, Coach, I just hope I can continue to do this for the rest of the season," James responded.

"It is going to get tougher, James. I am seriously thinking about moving you up to the varsity team," Coach Alexander said. "I need another good wrestler at the 112-pound weight class, and I think you will do well."

"Wow, Coach, do you really think I am that good?"

"Hell, yeah, you are going to be a very good wrestler," Coach Alexander said. "I need to get you wrestling on the varsity team now so that you will be a state champion in the future."

"Johnny, did you hear that? Coach Alexander thinks I am good enough to be on the varsity team."

"Oh, yeah, I heard him. I told you that you have what it takes to be good," Johnny said. "If you believe that you are a good wrestler, you will be a good wrestler."

"You should have known that I would be pretty good at kicking ass and taking names," James said.

"Yeah, yeah, you sure did," Johnny said sarcastically.

Although James was doing well on the wrestling mat, he continued his disrespectful, intolerable behavior in the classroom. Over the course of the school year, James was suspended from school nine times for fighting with the other students or disrespecting his teachers. However, he did manage to have a winning record of 7-2 on the wrestling team and get promoted to the tenth grade.

Reginald was having his way on the basketball court. During an introduction of the starting lineup for Reginald's first game, he received a standing ovation from the crowd. The gymnasium was packed to capacity for the first junior varsity basketball game. Reginald was the starting shooting guard and led his team to a 65-48 victory over Fredrick High School. James and Stacy were on hand watching, and congratulated Reginald after the game.

"Hey, man, you played one hell of a game tonight," James said.

"I really appreciate that coming from you, since I use to play behind you in middle school," Reginald said.

"Yeah, but you are much better than I am now," James said.

Reginald became very popular with his classmates, and was ultimately selected as the pride and joy of the freshman class. By sophomore year, Reginald continued to gain popularity among the coaching staff as well as the student body. He was so popular, that he smooth talked his way into the womanhood of one of the seniors at the school.

"Leslie, what's up, girl?" Reginald asked.
"I don't know, handsome, what's up with you?" Leslie responded.
"I was wondering, am I to young for you?"
"Yeah, boy, but you are just so cute."
"I hate the fact that the women I like don't seem to like me," Reginald said with a puppy dog look on his face. "I like you so much, why won't you be with me?"
"Well, it's not that I don't like you, because I do, but you are just so young and I have a boyfriend."
"Well all right, I just want you to know that you hurt my feelings," Reginald said looking down at the floor.
"What are you going to be doing after school today?" Leslie asked.
"I don't know, why do you ask?"
"Can you meet me in the gym at six o'clock?"
"Why?" Reginald asked, looking confused.
"Just meet me there at six o'clock, and you will see," Leslie said as she turned and walked away.
Reginald stood there in a daze for a couple of minutes. He did not know what was going on. He yelled for Leslie to come back, but she continued to walk away. He could not concentrate on his schoolwork for the rest of the day. He had no clue as to what was in store for him at six o'clock. After school, he noticed that it was a few minutes after six, so he nervously headed to the gym.
"For a minute there, I thought you weren't coming," Leslie said.
"Well, I'm here now, what's going on?" Reginald asked still looking confused.
"Everyone is gone now. I want you to come with me downstairs to the locker room so I can show you something."
"Okay," he said as he swallowed and took a deep breath.
Once the two were downstairs in the locker room, Leslie pulled up her dress, took off her panties and told Reginald, "I can't wait to feel you inside of me."
"But I don't have a condom on me," Reginald said.
"Believe me, baby, I've gotten that all taken care of. I'm on the pill," Leslie said.

Reginald's eyes got as big as golf balls. He could feel the sweat forming on his forehead. His heart seemed to have jumped in his throat. He cleared his throat twice before speaking.

"Leslie, what are you doing? Someone might catch us," Reginald said as he looked around the locker room.

"Trust me, everyone's gone. I should know, I come here all the time," Leslie said as she pushed Reginald up against the lockers.

Leslie started kissing Reginald on the lips as she asked, "Do you want me baby?" while unbuttoning his shirt and pants.

"Yes," Reginald said, stuttering.

"I want you so bad," Leslie said as she started groping Reginald's private parts.

Reginald couldn't believe how his manhood started expanding at the touch of Leslie's hand rubbing the outside of his jeans. Leslie threw Reginald's shirt on the bench behind them and slowly peeled his pants down. With his jeans down around his ankles, Leslie led Reginald to the end of the bench. She took a step back, pulled her blue jean dress over her head and stood before him in all of her glory. Reginald blinked several times, thinking this must be a dream. Leslie had the perfect body. She had the prototypical gymnast body. Her breasts were so round and perky, that she didn't need a bra to hold them up. After she flung her dress to the floor, Leslie stepped toward Reginald and pulled his underwear down so that they were joining his jeans around his ankles. She gave Reginald a slight push for him to sit on the edge of the bench.

Reginald was so bewildered, that he did not know what to do with his hands. Leslie took Reginald's right hand and put it between her legs.

"Oh, Leslie, you are as wet as a flowing river," Reginald said as Leslie rubbed her hands through Reginald's curly brown hair.

"Just relax, baby," Leslie said as she straddled him and placed his hands on her hips.

"Reginald, you have got me so excited," Leslie said as she placed his manhood inside of her and began riding him like he was a stallion. After a few minutes, Reginald practically lost his mind.

"Oh, Leslie, your body is so beautiful and this feels so good," Reginald said as his eyes lit up with excitement as he began to climax.

"Oh, Reginald, you're making me cum," Leslie screamed as she started to tremble frantically.

The two held each other for a few minutes after the encounter. "Now that wasn't so bad, was it?" Leslie asked as she proceeded to get off Reginald and began putting on her clothes.

"No, as a matter of fact, that was the best feeling I have ever had," Reginald replied.

"Well, you know Carlos is my boyfriend, but I will sneak around with you anytime."

"Well, maybe we can do it again sometime," Reginald said calmly.

The next day, Reginald walked around school with all of the confidence in the world. He had his eye on a young lady that he was very much infatuated with. Her name was Tameka Sanders and she was considered by many to be the prettiest girl in the sophomore class. Many of the students in the class said that they would be the perfect couple. All of the guys wanted to date Tameka and all of the girls wanted to date Reginald. One day, Reginald finally got up the nerve to ask Tameka to be his girlfriend.

"Tameka, can I talk to you for a minute?"

"Sure, Reginald, what is it?"

"I wondered if I could call you sometime?"

"Why would you want to call me?" Tameka asked.

"Because I think you are very pretty, and I wondered if you would be my girlfriend?"

Tameka was so flattered that she could not respond for a few seconds. "Yes, Reginald, I will be your girlfriend. I just can't believe you asked me. So many girls would love to be your girlfriend, why me?"

"I have been crazy about you for a long time. I was afraid for whatever reason that you might not like me."

"Hell, everybody likes you. You have made me the happiest girl in the world," Tameka said.

Reginald approached Tameka and kissed her on the lips. Tameka kept the biggest smile on her face for the rest of the day.

In the ensuing weeks, James and Reginald did not spend as much time together anymore due to Reginald's undivided attention to Tameka. Anyone could clearly see that Reginald was very much in love. He went everywhere with Tameka. Outside of school and basketball, Reginald started spending practically every day with her. He would wait until his parents made plans for the evening to go out, and then invite Tameka over to his house.

"Hello, may I speak to Tameka?" Reginald would ask.

"This is she, how are you doing baby?"

"I'm okay. My folks are going out tonight. Can you get one of your friends to bring you over here?"

"I think so. I will just tell my parents I am going over to my friend Lisa's house to study. They like Lisa and she always covers for me."

"Okay, well, they will be leaving in a few minutes so come on over."

"I'll be there as soon as I can, baby. Good-bye."

Reginald's parents went out dancing at least once a week. Whenever Tameka would go to Reginald's house, they would have sex all over the house. He would tell James and Stacy that he and Tameka would always take a shower together, then kiss and caress each other all the way to the bedroom. Once Reginald bragged to James and Stacy about how great sex was, and how sexy Tameka was in the nude.

"James, Tameka and I are going to get married someday."

"Why do you say that, man?" James asked.

"Because Tameka is so beautiful and I really enjoy having sex with her."

"I hope you want to marry her for more than just sex?" James asked.

"Yeah, I was just kidding, I think she's a smart girl, too."

"That's better, I thought you were loosing it for a minute there."

James managed to get suspended from school eleven times for a number of reasons, but mainly for fighting. One particular young lady that James wanted to date was the lovely Olivia Harper. Olivia had an almond complexion with shoulder length hair and round cheeks with the deepest dimples that gave her the greatest sex appeal. She was definitely all woman. With her well-shaped buttocks and large breasts, James was very infatuated with her body. However, Olivia, like the other girls in school, considered James to be too vicious to ever want to have a relationship with him. One of the most common comments made about him was that he was "deranged." James happened to get Olivia's telephone number from a friend and called her. James wore his heart on his sleeve by letting her know that he liked her, but was rejected yet again. She told James that the only way she would ever consider being with him was if he no longer went to the same school as she and her friends. James was hurt deeply, but still had feelings for her. By his sophomore year, James acquired a new friend named Lewis Clark. Lewis and James became good friends because they were on the wrestling team together. Lewis had attended Sego Middle School, but he and James barely knew each other then.

Stacy was now dating Shayna Butler who had blossomed into a sexy teenage girl. Shayna was now a beautiful high school debutante and would tell all of her friends that she was very much in love with Stacy. Stacy treated Shayna as if she were a princess. One day while the two were on a break between classes, Stacy asked Shayna what she wanted to do after school that day.

"Oh, I don't know, why do you ask?" Shayna replied.

"I was hoping we could go to the mall and do some shopping," Stacy said. "I need to buy myself another pair of tennis shoes."

"Okay, are you going to give me a ride home?"

"No, I'm going to leave you at the mall," Stacy said sarcastically.

"Whatever you want to do, honey, is okay with me. As long as I am with you, I'm happy."

"I love you, Shayna."

"I love you, too, Stacy."

"Meet me at my car after school," Stacy said.

"I'll be there," Shayna said as she batted her baby brown eyes at him.

After school, the two met at Stacy's car. Shayna was so hot for Stacy that she practically undressed him before they got into the car. She was kissing all over him like he had just returned home from Vietnam. After several failed attempts, Stacy was finally able to get her into the car. Once inside the car, Shayna reached over and put her hand on Stacy's thigh as they traveled to Lennox Square Mall.

"We will only be in here for a little while," Stacy said as they entered the mall parking lot.

"No rush, baby, I can call my mom and let her know that I am with you, so take your time. We don't have to rush home."

"Okay, because you know my mother lets me do whatever I want to. She gave me forty dollars this morning and told me to have a nice day. As soon as you get off the phone, we can go and get something to eat. I'm hungry," Stacy said.

"Okay. I'll only be a minute," Shayna said.

"What did she say?" Stacy asked as Shayna hung up the telephone.

"She told me to tell you hello, and that she was going to the store. She told me that if we wanted to catch a movie or something while we were here, it was okay with her."

"Boy, your mother is really cool," Stacy said. "She is almost as cool as my mother."

"See, I told you not to worry," Shayna said.

"Well, come on. Let me get my shoes and something to eat and then we can go to the theater and see what's playing."

After the couple had finished their shopping and getting a bite to eat, they decided that they did not want to go to the movies. Instead they decided to take a romantic walk through Chastain Park.

While walking through the park, Shayna began groping Stacy's buttocks. Stacy had never seen her act like this before so he started getting suspicious.

"Shayna, why are you acting like this?"

"Because I love you, Stacy, and I want to make love to you."

"Have you lost your mind? We can't have sex outside in the broad day light."

"I know, I just want you so bad right now," Shayna said. "I have been thinking about this ever since you told me to meet you at the car."

"Yeah, but I meant wait until we get to my house because my mother is out of town until tomorrow."

"Okay, can we go to your house now?" Shayna asked. "I'll try to wait until we get to your house."

"Sure if you want to go," Stacy responded.

Stacy was so excited that he did not say a word the entire twenty minute drive. Once they reached the house, the couple went inside. Shayna asked Stacy if she could freshen up. "Sure, let me get you a wash cloth and a towel," he said. Shayna was taking a shower when there was a knock on the bathroom door.

"Yes," Shayna said trying to hurry, anticipating what was to come.

"Do you want me to join you in the shower?" Stacy asked.

"No, I'll be out in a minute."

"Okay," Stacy said as he headed to his room that was adjacent to the bathroom.

When Shayna finished her shower, she wrapped herself in the towel that Stacy had given her. She opened the bathroom door and headed toward the living room when she heard Stacy call, "Shayna, I'm in here."

"Oh there you are," Shayna said as she entered the bedroom.

Stacy's manhood began to extend at the site of his beautiful girlfriend and the thought of what was yet to come.

"Are you nervous?" Shayna asked when she noticed that Stacy had gotten under the covers.

"A little. How about you?" Stacy asked clearing his throat.

"Not at all. I have been dreaming about this day."

Stacy didn't say a word as he began to lick his lips. Shayna joined him in the bed as she began to undress him. He acted as if he was paralyzed. After he assisted Shayna in taking off his clothes, he didn't move a muscle or say a word. Shayna was obviously no stranger to the world of sex. She pulled the white comforter off the bed and told Stacy to lay on his back and move to the center of the bed. After Stacy was in the center of the bed, she kissed him from head to toe, lingering at his manhood.

Shayna dropped her bath towel and climbed on top of Stacy. Their kisses were long and full, leaving him dreaming and fluttering beneath her. Small droplets of sweat fell from her forehead to his face, leaving little pockets of coldness that felt pleasantly wet. Her mouth teased his ears until his damp brown flesh became warm, and her hand gripped the top of the bed sheet pulling it slowly down. As he pulled her close, their lean, slender bodies joined together easily, so easily that she felt she must have known him forever. The movements awakened him and brought him into an unfamiliar territory. This was real, this is what could still the longing in his heart. Her rhythm grew more intense and more savage as she rose up and down above him, imprisoning him in her grasp. He let the thrust overpower him until nothing else existed for him in the world. The sight of his face weak with emotion, yet ferocious with need, was so awesome that she stared at it in wonder until his wave of feelings crested and left him frail. When he opened his eyes, falling slowly back to earth, he saw that she had been watching him in enchantment, her eyes raking his body with raw gratification. He was filled with a sudden, reckless need to overpower her in return and before she knew what was happening, he had flipped her over, and was on top of her, teasing, pushing and encouraging her until her fist grasped the sheets and her body tensed in expectation. He entered her and savored the final, uncontrollable moment when she trembled into oblivion, and then they were lying in each other's arms, victorious, and tired.

Shayna asked, "Are you ready to take me home, baby?"

"Not really, but I know your mother will start to worry about you if I don't take you home now."

Stacy and Shayna continued their relationship throughout the school year, but saw less of each other once summer started. During the summer of their sophomore year, James was able to get a job at McDonald's, Reginald worked as a lifeguard at one of the city swimming pools and Stacy continued to sit around the house watching television. At the end of the summer, after saving his money from his job, James was able to buy a few pairs of nice pants, a few shirts, and couple of pairs of nice shoes. He also bought three pairs of jeans and three shirts for his brother Jeff, who was too young to work at the time. He was able to save four hundred dollars that he gave to his mother to keep for him. Reginald's parents told him that the money he made, he could keep as spending money, and that they would buy his clothes and a car when he returned to school. Stacy's mother purchased him a beautiful two door, gold colored Honda Accord.

One day in a casual conversation, James and his father made a pact that whatever money James saved from working at McDonald's, his dad would match that amount in order to help James procure a car. At the end of the summer, Michael matched his four hundred dollars. Again, James gave the money to his mother and asked her to keep it until he found a car that he could buy.

About a week and a half later, Carolyn was in an automobile accident. About two weeks after the accident, she bought a beautiful sky blue Cadillac Deville.

Approximately three weeks after the accident, Michael did not know that Carolyn had purchased another car and he gave her twelve hundred dollars for a down payment to get another car. He made it clear that he had forgiven her for not allowing him to raise the children, and that he thought that she should have dependable transportation.

When James returned to school the following day, Stacy told him that he was selling his Honda Accord for eight hundred dollars. When James got home, he ran to his mother with what he thought was good news. When he asked Carolyn for his money, she told him that she had spent his money on bills.

James could not believe his mother would do that to him. He cried for a week about that car. Michael was furious because he had given James the money but didn't see a car. He believed that James had lied about saving money and that he just wanted to swindle money out of him. James was afraid to tell his father what his mother did because she threatened to whip him if he told his father.

James was now under the watchful eye of the principal because of all of the trouble he had caused over the previous two years. After James was suspended for the fifth time during his junior year, the principal enlightened him that he would be expelled if he got into any more trouble. The principal went so far as to make James sign a contract stating that if he got into any more trouble, he would be expelled.

James D. Jackson, Ph.D.

There was a senior by the name of Alvin Tucker who really had it in for James. Alvin did not care for James because he thought that he was too crazy to remain in school.

Somehow, Alvin found out that James was on probation and thought that it would be a good idea to start a fight with him because he knew that if he fought back, he would be expelled.

"What's up punk?" Alvin would ask.

"Nothing man, I'm not looking for any trouble," James would respond.

"It doesn't matter, because I don't like your punk ass."

"Look, man, I am on probation, and if I get into a fight with anyone, I will get kicked out of school for good."

Alvin would kick or punch James to try to get into a fight with him. James was doing his best not to fight Alvin because he really wanted to stay at Brookview. It got so bad that Alvin had his best friend Robert help him jump on James and beat him up. Robert held James while Alvin kicked him in the face and ribs. James continued to take their abuse and would not fight back in fear of being kicked out of school.

It was now wintertime and basketball season was in session. Alvin Tucker was a member of the basketball team at Brookview. One day the basketball team traveled to play a game at another school. His car was parked in the parking lot in front of Brookview's gymnasium. The wrestling team concluded practice and headed for the showers. After their showers, the team headed outside to meet the late bus that would take them downtown to Five Points Station. When they got downtown, they would catch the bus that would take them home. Once the boys got outside the gym, James noticed Alvin Tucker's car parked in the parking lot. He stopped Lewis and a few of the other wrestlers and pointed at the car. They discussed how they were going to vandalize Alvin's car. James thought that flattening all four of the tires was a good idea and the other boys agreed. The boys thought that letting air out of the tires would be a good practical joke, but then things got out of hand. After the boys starting letting air out of the tires, they started kicking the car. Lewis smashed the front left and right headlights with a

Wrong Perception

brick that was lying on the ground, bent the license plate and all of the boys took turns spitting on the car.

"Ah, man, I did not tell you guys to break anything, now the cops are going to be called in," James said.

"Fuck it man, only wrestlers are out here, so who's going to tell?" Lewis said.

The next day James and a few of the boys involved decided that they would not go to school the following day so that they would not be questioned by anyone about the car.

One of the smallest wrestlers on the team, Tim Wilson, was not involved in the incident. He was questioned by the police. The police threatened to take him downtown and arrest him if he knew something and did not come forward. Tim was so afraid of being arrested that he told the police what happened. James was at home thinking that everything was okay when the telephone rang. He received a call at his home from the principal informing him that an eyewitness just told the police what happened and the sheriff was en route to his house to pick him up. The principal told James to gather all of his books and anything else that belonged to the school and be prepared to turn it in when he arrived, because he was certainly going to be expelled. James' mother was phoned by the school and informed of what happened and was told that she needed to meet the police at the school. Carolyn left her job and headed to the school. Once she and James arrived at the school, the principal explained again what happened and informed her that James was expelled. Carolyn went crazy, she must have slapped James at least ten times before the principal could jump in and restrain her. When James got home, his mother whipped him for the next three days. She would whip him until she got tired, take a coffee break and whip him again. James's mother, father, sister and brothers practically disowned him after the incident. His sister commented to her mother, "Three out of four ain't bad, you still have three good kids, Mom."

James had to appear in juvenile court to pay restitution for the damages. James's mother paid $200 and told James that he would be on punishment for the next six weeks.

After leaving juvenile court, James had a rendezvous with the superintendent of the Atlanta public school system. Mr.

Thomas Jordan, the superintendent, was a big black man, about 6'2" and weighing about 220 pounds.

"Boy, do you know the magnitude of an education? If you don't graduate from high school, this world is going to kick your ass. I am going to give you one more chance, do you understand?" Mr. Thomas asked.

"Yes, sir, I understand," James responded.

"If you get emancipated from another high school in Atlanta, you are going to be forbidden to attend any other school in the city."

"I am going to stay out of trouble so I can graduate from high school," James said.

James was enrolled in Charles High School. It was located only a couple of blocks from his house. Charles High did not have the financial support from the state that Brookview had. Charles High was not that competitive academically either. Most of the students that received scholarships to college after high school were usually athletes. Socially, Charles High did not present the same fortune that Brookview had—performing arts and a wrestling team. Charles High was comprised of students whose families were very indigent or from the lower middle class, virtually all African-American students. Whereas Brookview High was an amalgam of students that came from lower and upper class families.

After being told by his mother that he would be kicked out of the house and sent to boarding school if he got suspended just once from Charles High, James decided to concentrate on graduating rather than being the class bully. He also realized that Charles was a school made up primarily of students from lower class families that were inclined to fight as groups rather than as individuals.

On the first day of school, James witnessed a fight between a student named Duane who lived in a neighborhood not far from his house and another student named Eric from one of Atlanta's housing developments. Eric was initially loosing the fight, but once members of the housing development realized he was in a fight, at least twelve of his neighbors got involved and inevitably kicked Duane in the head and chest until he went into a coma.

Wrong Perception

The students from the housing development were so out of control that many of the kicks occurred while the principal of the school was standing over Duane's body. James knew that being the class bully at Charles High could literally get him killed. He was sure that he did not want what happened to Duane happening to him.

On the second day of school, James arrived at his sixth period class before many of the other students when one of the students approached him and said, "Hey man, you need to get up and sit somewhere else."

"I'm not moving anywhere. You better find somewhere else to sit," James responded.

The student's name was Kevin Beasley and although he'd never met James before, he immediately didn't like him.

Kevin decided that he would not try to fight James but wouldtell the class bully a lie. The class bully at Charles High was Michael Conrad. Michael was not from the housing development that many of the students were from. However, he had many friends from the housing development so when he got in a fight at school, no one would get involved. He was actually a year behind in school, and was a year older than the other students in his class. Michael was the only student in the junior class that could bench press 315 pounds.

Kevin told Michael that James was going around school telling everyone that he was a punk. Michael was so angry at what Kevin was telling him that on the third day of school, he walked up to James and punched him in the face. James was stunned, he didn't know what in the hell was going on.

"Why in the world did you hit me?" James asked.

"You just better not say that shit again," Michael responded.

As Michael started to walk away, a few of the girls in the school approached James and told him, "Michael is jealous because you look better than he does."

"I sure hope that isn't the case. There are a lot of ugly people at this school," James responded.

James was very upset and did not have a clue about what had just transpired. The principal heard about the episode and called James and Michael to his office. James arrived at the principal's office first. The principal asked James what happened and he explained that he did not know why Michael Conrad punched him in the face. When Michael finally arrived, the principal asked him what happened. Michael stated that James was going around telling everybody that he was a punk. James told Michael that he had never seen him before so how could he have said that to anyone. That was when Michael told James that Kevin Beasley had given him the erroneous information. At first James told Michael that he did not know anyone named Kevin Beasley. Michael explained to James that he was in his sixth period class and described him to James. Then James recalled the incident that prompted the attack.

James and Michael shook hands and put the incident behind them, but Michael was suspended for three days. Michael was a linebacker on the football team and was considerably bigger than most of the students that attended the school.

James did not play baseball during his junior year at Charles High because he was ineligible. He now had more time to spend on his schoolwork and the lovely Olivia Harper that was now calling him. She held true to her statement that she would talk to him once he no longer went to the same school as she did. James and Olivia would meet any place they could without being seen by others. The place they considered to be their place was a beautiful and exclusive spot at the lake. One day after school, James and Olivia agreed to meet at their spot. Olivia told her parents that she would be home late because she had to do some research for a term paper, and James told his mother that he was going to watch the guys practice for the upcoming baseball game. James arrived first and laid out a blanket, he hid the blanket behind the bushes before he went to school and got it on his way to the lake. James was sitting on the blanket watching the still water when Olivia came up from behind him. She covered his eyes and gently kissed him on the ear. James reached behind him, pulled Olivia into his lap and began kissing and caressing her. This was both James and Olivia's first time and both were very nervous. James slowly unbuttoned her shirt and began kissing and softly licking Olivia's now exposed breasts. Olivia moaned in a low, soft whimper. Passion consumed Olivia and she removed James' black T-shirt and unzipped his jeans. Olivia was wearing a blue skirt and James ran his hand slowly up her thigh and pulled down her panties. James was now rushing to get his pants down, he couldn't wait to feel what a woman felt like. He finally got his pants down and started moving towards her with his dick standing at attention, when she stopped him.

"James, do you have a condom with you?" Olivia asked with her hands on James's chest, slightly pushing him back.

"Of course I do, it's in my wallet," James said looking for his jeans. James got his wallet out of his pants pocket and took the condom out showing Olivia the small Trojan packet.

"You only have one?" Olivia asked.

"No, but all I need is one," James said with a confused look on his face.

"Yeah, but one condom only gives you 80 percent protection," Olivia said.

"Okay, I'll use two and that will give us 160 percent protection," James said reaching in his wallet for another condom.

"Well, if you use two condoms we can do this," Olivia said.

"Oh, all right."

James put on two condoms to please Olivia. While she was lying on her back, James slowly spread her thighs and put his well-covered penis into Olivia's womanhood. James had no sensation whatsoever, but Olivia seemed to enjoy herself very much. She was moaning something awful. She called out James's name and told James that she did not want him to ever have sex with anyone else. When the unpleasant experience for James was over, he slowly got up. He took the condoms off and tossed them in the trash can that was two trees to the right of them. James put on his clothes not saying a word. While Olivia was putting on her clothes, she asked, "Did you enjoy it, because I did?"

"Yes, I enjoyed myself very much," James lied.

"When will I see you again?" Olivia asked.

"I'm not sure. I'll call you," James said.

He didn't want to hurt her feelings, but that was one of the most miserable experiences of James's life. They walked together not saying a word and once they came to the halfway point, they parted and went their separate ways. Olivia attempted to call

James a few times after the sexual encounter. James was so rude to her, that she stopped calling him for good.

When James was expelled from Brookview High, he had received five failing grades on his report card and had to attend summer school to make up those classes. James enrolled in those classes at Frederick Taylor High School where summer school was being held. James was able to pass four of the five classes he was taking in summer school and was on track to graduate with his class.

Reginald was now playing basketball for Brookview High. He was the starting shooting guard on the team. Reginald was having a difficult time trying to decide what girl he wanted to be with. He had a girlfriend at three different high schools in Atlanta. Stacy and Reginald would normally double date taking their girlfriends to the movies or to restaurants after school. During Reginald's junior year at Brookview, he was converted from a running back to a defensive back. The head coach at Brookview thought that Reginald was too small to be an offensive player, but would be prototypical for the defensive backfield. During his junior year, he shared time with a senior at cornerback. By his senior year, he was a starter. Newberry University sent scouts to watch Reginald play in his last game of his senior year. Reginald played one of the best games of his life. He was able to intercept two passes and return them both for touchdowns. He was recognized by the *Atlanta Constitution* as the player of the week. Reginald had taken his football game to the next level. The scouts were so impressed with him that Newberry offered him a full athletic scholarship and he accepted. Reginald made a composite score of 850 on the SAT and possessed a cumulative GPA of 2.6. He was fully qualified to take the scholarship. In his honor, his family held a surprise party for him, for this accomplishment.

Reginald and Stacy managed to keep in contact with James during the remainder of their senior year. James tried out for Charles High's baseball team during his senior year and was selected to play. He was able to raise his cumulative GPA from a 1.76 to a 2.01 and lead his team with eight homeruns at the end of the season. James had such an outstanding season at Charles

High that he, along with his teammate Joseph Austin, received a letter from the head baseball coach at Alabama State University, inviting them to Alabama State to play baseball, and they accepted. The coach informed James that he would not be able to give him a scholarship due to his grades and low SAT score. He'd only scored a composite score of 640 on the SAT. In addition, he'd be required to take developmental studies classes at Alabama State University.

At Reginald's high school graduation, the principal made public that Reginald was one of only two student athletes to receive a full athletic scholarship to college. He was the envy of all those who weren't as auspicious.

The day after Reginald's graduation, James called him and Stacy on the telephone and asked if they wanted to go to Barton Chapel Elementary School to reminisce and later to a club. They all agreed that they would like to go to the school first and then to a nightclub. Reginald was to pick up James and Stacy sometime between seven and seven-thirty.

When Reginald arrived at each of the boy's homes, they were outside waiting for him. When the friends made it to the school, they decided to sit on the swings before inaugurating their discussion. As the friends sat on the swings, they reminisced about old times and talked about their unfolding goals.

Reginald brought his class yearbook with him when the boys met at the school.

"Hey, man let me see your yearbook," James asked, swinging around in the swing with his hands stretched out for the book.

"Here you go but be careful not to bend the pages I'm on," Reginald said flipping up his collar and showing all thirty-two.

While looking through the yearbook, James noticed in the superlative section of the yearbook that Reginald was voted most attractive, most likely to succeed and the best male athlete in the senior class. After looking through the yearbook, the boys fondly recalled their younger days, remembering the girls that took their virginity.

"Do you guys remember Shayna Butler, well, man, she really put it on me. When she was done with me, I swore I needed a bib. I was dribbling all over myself," Stacy said with a far off look in his eyes.

"Yeah, I know what you mean. Leslie wore me out in the boys' locker room," Reginald said clearing his throat and now tugging on his collar.

"I don't care to talk about my two condom-wearing experience," James said as the boys laughed in unison.

"I think I really want to be a professional football player," Reginald said.

"I think I want to own my own business," Stacy replied.

"I'm sure that I want to be a professional baseball player," James said.

After they reminisced about the days gone by and their future plans, they noticed that it was now 10 P.M. and time to go to the club. At the club, the friends enjoyed themselves very much. They flirted with every lady in the place. After several hours, they decided that they had endured enough and it was time to go home. On the way home, Stacy mentioned that he had decided that he wanted to attend Newberry University because he did not want to be away from Reginald. He applied to Newberry a few days later and was accepted.

8

Choices

In the fall of 1985, the guys went away to school. During the fall, ASU held tryouts and James was selected to be one of the pitchers on the varsity baseball team. While at Newberry Reginald worked so hard during the summer to get ready for football season that he moved into the starting line-up after the third week of summer practice. He was able to remain healthy the entire season and instantly gained the respect of his teammates and coaches. The first quarter went by quickly and it was time for the guys to go home for the Christmas holidays.

During the Christmas holiday season when Reginald and Stacy stopped by the Jones' residence to see James, Reginald shared his "player of the week" newspaper article with him. The article mentioned that Reginald made three interceptions against one of the school's rival colleges. James told Reginald that he was very proud of how well he was doing at Newberry. The friends talked about their first quarter of college and how they missed hanging out together.

"Man, I never knew that college life would be so much fun," James said. "There is a party practically every weekend and there are fine motherfuckers on every corner you turn."

"I know that's right," Stacy said. "We have a nine to one, girl to guy ratio."

"So not only do I have my nine, but there are a couple of faggots at Newberry, so you know I have their nine too," Reginald said as the fellows laughed.

"I think I have had sex with about fifteen girls already," James said. "I don't know how I could ever graduate from college having this much fun."

"I know that's right," Stacy said.

"At my school, if you buy a girl a box of chicken, you're in there," James said as the boys laughed.

"James, have you gotten into any fights yet?" Reginald asked sarcastically.

"Not yet," James replied.

"I miss the good old days," Reginald said. "What are Gina, Johnny and Jeff doing these days?"

"Johnny is a sophomore at the University of Georgia, majoring in Aeronautics, Gina is a junior at Clark-Atlanta University, majoring in broadcast journalism, and Jeff is in his senior year at Brookview."

"What about Monique, what is she doing now?" James asked.

"She was working for a doctor downtown, but she got fired last month after being seen kissing another woman in the restroom."

"Is Monique a lesbian?" James asked.

"I guess so, man. Her damn girlfriend is working for my dad at the housing authority," Reginald replied.

"How about Victor, what is he doing now, Stacy?" James asked.

"Same old shit. Living at home with mom, hanging with his friend until the wee hours in the morning."

When Reginald returned to school for the winter and spring quarter, he managed to keep his GPA at 3.25. During the summer, he was practicing football with the team, eager to start his sophomore year. At the end of summer practice, there was a two-week break before school started.

James continued to work and play baseball, but his grades were getting worse. It was now the end of the spring quarter and time to go home for summer break. When James got home for summer vacation, he decided to teach himself all of the subjects that he knew were important for school. He purchased books at Waldenbooks that taught him how to write grammatically correct sentences and another book that covered the fundamentals of mathematics. For at least six hours per day for the entire summer, James studied and actually taught himself math and English. James also studied the dictionary, setting the

Wrong Perception

goal of learning at least four new words per day. He still enjoyed skating and continued skating when he returned home for summer break.

When Reginald returned to Newberry for his sophomore year he was approached by a young man named Terry Jones. Terry was a local drug dealer who lived near the campus. He was not a student, but spent a lot of time on campus.

"Reginald, do you know who I am?" Terry asked.

"No, I don't think I do," Reginald replied.

"I work around here, and I make a lot of money," Terry said. "You like money don't you?"

"Sure I do. You need money to live," Reginald said.

"What do you think about working for me on a part-time basis and making a lot of money?" Terry asked.

"Well, it depends on what kind of work it is," Reginald said with a curious look on his face, wondering what kind of business could this man have.

"Well, it's not back-breaking work if that's what you're asking," Terry said.

"Well, tell me, what kind of business do you have, and what would I be doing?" Reginald asked.

"With your popularity, the sky is the limit to the money you can make selling cocaine to the other students." At first Reginald told Terry that he did not want to get involved with something like that, but when Terry showed Reginald eight thousand dollars in cash, he changed his mind.

"How can I sell the drugs without getting caught by the police?" Reginald asked.

"You would only deal for about two months because of your popularity," Terry said.

"What does my popularity have to do with it?" Reginald asked.

"Reginald, you can get a lot of the other students to distribute the drugs for you because they like and respect you so much."

"How do you know all this?"

"I notice how they look up to you because of your looks and athletic ability. Let's face it, everyone in college is broke and everyone is looking to have a good time," Terry said with a grin on his face. "Would you agree or disagree with that statement."

"Yes, I agree," Reginald said, looking around to see if anyone was listening.

"So, tell me pretty boy, are you in or out?" Terry asked.

"Count me in. Lord knows I need the money," Reginald said.

Initially, Reginald did not tell Stacy, but when he finally did, Stacy thought it was a good business venture and decided to become a part of it.

Reginald began selling drugs in January of 1987. Stacy started selling drugs in the middle of February that same year. They set out to make as much money as they could.

During the winter, while attending ASU, James was able to thumb a ride home to see his family. When he got home, he noticed a gold Honda Accord in the driveway. When he opened the door and went inside, he noticed that only his younger brother Jeff was at home.

"Jeff, whose car is that parked in the driveway?" James asked.

"It's mine, mom bought it for me," Jeff said with a big smile on his face, trying to rub it in.

"What the fuck do you mean she bought it for you?" James asked with anger in his voice because his mother never did any thing for him.

"Like I said man, mom got it for me," Jeff repeated.

James was so angry that he got back into the car with the person that brought him home, and asked if he could take him to his father's house. James's friend said that he would and away they went.

When James arrived at his father's house, he asked if he would buy him a car. Michael told James that he was still upset with him about the money he gave him for the last car. However, he had an old station wagon that he was looking to give away. The station wagon was sky blue with no hubcaps, rust spots and dents all over it from previous accidents. Michael told James that he could have the old station wagon, if he wanted it, or he would give it to someone off the street. James decided to take the car

Wrong Perception

and head back to school because he was too angry to go back to his mother's. He was afraid of what he might say to Carolyn.

During the spring of 1987 while at ASU, James got a surprise visit. James and one of the other baseball players were standing outside the student center talking to two young ladies. A red convertible 325 BMW with tinted windows pulled up. All of the students outside the student center focused their attention on the red sports car. The car stopped and the door opened. To James's surprise, it was his longtime friends, Reginald and Stacy. Reginald called James over and they hugged one another.

"Hey, boy what's going on?" Reginald asked.

"I don't know, you tell me. You are the one that is on my campus."

"I came to see you, man. Is that okay?"

"You know I am always glad to see you and Stacy."

"We just wanted to come see you and tell you what we have been up to."

"I'm really glad to see you guys. It's strange how we go from seeing each other every day, to seeing each other once a year."

"James, have you eaten yet?" Stacy asked.

"No, not yet, why do you ask?"

"We are starving. Where are the restaurants around here?"

"All of the restaurants are within ten to fifteen minutes from here."

"Buddy-boy, Stacy and I have something we need to discuss with you. So pick any restaurant that you want to go to, it will be my treat."

"Well let's go to Red Lobster."

Once the friends got to Red Lobster, Reginald asked for a booth in the corner. At that time, James commented to Reginald and Stacy about how good they looked with the fancy clothes and jewelry. Reginald then asked James how he was doing and he told him that it was very difficult playing baseball, working a part-time job, going to school and trying to maintain his grades. James told Reginald and Stacy that he was a stock boy in a local grocery store making minimum wage and that his grades weren't that good. He told his friends that the very attractive girls would not give him the time of day because he didn't wear name brand clothes and drive a nice car, but stated that he did get some play from the average chicks. Just as Reginald started to explain to James why they had come to talk to him, the waitress arrived and asked if they were ready to order.

"Are you gentlemen ready to order?" the waitress asked.

"James, order any and everything you want," Reginald told him.

"What's up man, are you loaded or something?" James asked.

"Yeah, you can say that," Reginald responded.

"In that case I'll have the trout and shrimp combo, tossed salad with blue cheese dressing and a glass of sweet tea.

"And you sir?" the waitress asked, looking at Reginald.

"I'll have the lobster, a baked potato with butter and sour cream, a tossed salad with ranch dressing and a glass of red wine," Reginald said.

"I'll have the same thing he's having," Stacy said pointing at Reginald.

"I'll be right back with your drinks and salads," the waitress said leaving the table.

"You know man, you don't have to keep living like this." Reginald said.

"What lottery am I going to win to change my situation?" James asked.

"Stacy and I are in business together, and we need another partner. Someone we can trust." Reginald went on to say that James too could have all the money, clothes, jewelry and pretty girls that he wanted.

"What type of business would afford me all of that?" James asked. Just as Reginald got ready to tell James what business they were in, the waitress returned with their food.

Over dinner, Reginald told James that he and Stacy were immersed in the distribution of narcotics and that he did not want to leave him out of an opportunity of a lifetime. James looked at Reginald with amazement because he thought that Reginald's mother and father were still giving him anything he wanted. Reginald told James that he did not have to answer right then, but that he and Stacy were going to be in town for a couple of days. After dinner the three friends got back in the car and

Wrong Perception

talked about old times as they headed back to the campus. When James got back to his room, his friends told him that they were going to check out the city for a few days and then they would be back to see him before they went back to South Carolina.

While lying in bed, James fantasized about all of the cars, money and girls he could have if he affiliated himself with the business. The next evening, while working stocking shelves, James realized that he wanted to prove to himself and his family and friends, that he could make it in this world by becoming prosperous legally.

A couple of days later, while resting in his room after a very grueling day unloading trucks and stocking shelves, James heard a knock at the door. James yelled to come in because he was too tired to get up and answer the door. Reginald and Stacy walked in. Reginald didn't even bother asking James how he was doing or anything, he got straight to the point.

"What is your decision, are you in or out?" Reginald asked and waited for James to reply.

"This is not the right road to be on. Even though it will give me the money that I so desperately want and need, I can't do it," James said with a serious look on his face.

Reginald then showed James ten thousand dollars in cash and asked, "Are you sure man? There is a lot more money to be made."

"Yes, my mind is made up," James said firmly.

"You are working a penny ante job and driving a beat up station wagon. You don't have the pretty girls on your jock or any money. Why don't you come in the business just to see if you would like it?" Reginald said.

"James, we really need you in the business," Stacy persisted.

"No thank you, but I really enjoyed seeing you guys again. Be careful and watch your backs because someone will always be after you," James said. He knew that this was probably the last time that he would see his friends for a long time.

• • •

Back in South Carolina, Reginald held a meeting in his home every Tuesday for all of the drug dealers that were a part of what he affectionately called "The Gang."

Reginald would lay out the plans and ask for suggestions from The Gang. He was always very intelligent, and with his stunning good looks, he could hold the attention of anyone listening. His focus was always expansion. He thought the bigger his venture, the harder it would be to target any one person. A clever deception to take the attention off himself. Reginald would normally address The Gang with his usual introduction, "Good morning, Gang. The baddest gang in South Carolina is alive and well. The surrounding territories will be ours. Believe in The Gang and we will rule the world."

"Stacy, is everyone present?" Reginald would ask.

"Yes they are, boss."

"Okay, how much money did we rake in this week?" Reginald asked, rubbing his hands together.

"The same as the previous weeks. A whole lot," Stacy would say as The Gang members laughed.

"Now I want to know, what is our goal this week?"

"To make a lot of money," The Gang would say in unison.

"You are my homeys. You know I'll do whatever I have to for my homeys," Reginald would say.

The Gang was very loyal to Reginald because they knew that he could flex a little muscle if he had to. He was so carefree that he would not be upset if someone had to destroy drugs to avoid arrest or was short on the cash that they owed him. He showed his members that if they were loyal to him then he was loyal to them. If any one in The Gang had a problem, he would help them any way he could.

Late one evening, one of The Gang members was banging on Reginald and Stacy's door. He was upset because one of their rivals was sleeping with his girlfriend. Both Reginald and Stacy got out of bed.

"Man, who in the hell could be at our door this late?" Reginald asked.

"I don't know, but I'm going to find out," Stacy said getting his gun and going to the door.

"Who is it?" Stacy asked.

"Man, it's me, Greg," he said, waiting for Stacy to open the door.

Wrong Perception

"It's Greg, man," Stacy said to Reginald.

"Let him in. It must be important if he's coming here this late," Reginald said, turning on the lights in the living room. Stacy opened the door to let Greg in the house.

"I'm sorry to be coming over so late, but you told us if we ever had a problem to come to you," Greg said still waiting by the door.

"You're right, I did say that, so come on in, have a seat and tell me what the trouble is," Reginald said.

"Man, one of our gang rivals by the name of T'Bone is sleeping with my girl Shawana, and I don't know how to handle the situation."

"Don't worry, just be here Thursday night at eleven o'clock and we'll take care of this matter," Reginald said as he got up and walked out of the room. Stacy saw Greg out and went back to bed.

On Thursday, Greg was at Reginald's at exactly eleven o'clock. When Greg entered the house he was greeted by Stacy, Reginald, and two of The Gang members, Austin and Raymond.

"Good, everyone is here now, we can get going," Reginald said leading the pack. Everyone followed him without asking questions. They got in the car and headed to the Elite Club where T'Bone hung out. When they got inside the club they saw him sitting in a booth in the back of the smoke-filled club. T'Bone didn't even notice Reginald and the other guys standing in front of him because he was to busy trying to get into the panties of the girl that was sitting with him.

"Excuse me Mr. T'Bone, may I speak to you outside for a moment, please?" Reginald asked.

"What is this about, man?" T'Bone asked, flashing a mouth full of gold teeth.

"This won't take long," Reginald said.

"Man, if you can't tell me in here what it's about then I don't need to know," T'Bone said, taking a puff of his cigarette.

Reginald signaled for his boys to help T'Bone out of his seat and to the parking lot. The others in the club knew the routine—see no evil, speak no evil and hear no evil. Once they had T'Bone out in the parking lot, Reginald instructed Raymond and Austin to put him in the car.

"Hey, man where are you taking me?" T'Bone asked with fear in his voice.

"Quiet!" Reginald demanded. Stacy drove to an abandoned warehouse where they usually made their drug deals. When they arrived at the site, Charles, another Gang member, was waiting for them. He had a table full of torture devices laid out and ready to use: a blow torch, a cigarette lighter, a sharp Army knife, a 9 millimeter hand gun, a box of salt, a pair of handcuffs, and rope. Austin and Raymond took T'Bone inside of the warehouse and handcuffed him to a chair and tied his legs to the chair legs. Reginald, Stacy and Greg were right behind them in the warehouse.

"Look, man, what ever I did, I'm sorry," T'Bone pleaded.

"Do you know why you're here?" Reginald asked.

"No, but what ever it is I'm sorry," T'Bone said again.

"You know about The Gang of course?" Reginald asked.

"Of course I do, who doesn't?" T'Bone stated. "Man, if someone told you I was trying to steal your customers, they lied," he said thinking that that was why he was there.

"This is not about customers!" Reginald yelled.

"Then what is this about?" T'Bone asked looking confused.

"This is about Shawana Perkins you punk ass nigga!" Greg stated.

"Come on, man, all this is not necessary over a piece of pussy," T'Bone stated.

"It is more than necessary, it'll show the rest of you punk asses that you can't mess with The Gang's ladies," Reginald said, having a seat fifteen feet in front of T'Bone with the other members surrounding him like he was the president.

"Handle your business, Greg," Reginald stated as he and the others looked on.

Greg instructed Charles and Raymond to remove T'Bone's shirt and to gag him. T'Bone sat there gagged, handcuffed and tied to the chair. Greg picked up the knife and made small cuts all over T'Bone's chest and took salt and rubbed it into his open wounds. Tears streamed down T'Bone's face as he tried to endure the excruciating pain.

Wrong Perception

"Did you enjoy fucking my girl!" Greg screamed. T'Bone closed his eyes and all anyone could hear were the muffed sounds he was making. The others continued to watch as Greg had fun torching T'Bone.

"Clean this mess up, untie T'Bone, and let's get out of here," Reginald said as he got up to walked outside to the car.

"You heard him," Stacy yelled and quickly followed Reginald. The other members cleaned the place and left T'Bone sitting in the chair. The next day the word on the street was to stay away from any girl that dates someone in The Gang.

Business could not have been better for Reginald and Stacy. They had more money than they knew what to do with. Reginald had so much money coming in that that he could afford a new car every month and spend time every Monday getting a massage. He always told The Gang that if they needed him for something to make sure that they didn't bother him at his Monday 10 A.M. massage.

Reginald and Stacy were roommates living in a beautiful home. Reginald had two females, Jackie and Kim, who would massage him for about an hour every Monday.

"Mr. Maynard, this is Kim calling, how are you today?"

"I'm okay, what's going on?"

"I was calling to make sure we were still on for Monday at ten o'clock?"

"I am looking forward to it."

"Okay, you know my boss always wants me to call by midweek to find out if our customers are going to keep their appointments. You know we have people calling in all the time."

"Well, you know I understand business. You do what you got to do."

Stacy enjoyed spending his Mondays in his Jacuzzi with women at his command. You could always find Stacy in their home by the smell of the cigars he enjoyed so much. Reginald had two Rottweilers and Stacy had one Doberman Pinscher. Reginald would have never imagined in his wildest dreams that being a star football player at the university was going to build him a huge drug distributorship. Reginald and Stacy were having the time of their lives in South Carolina.

James D. Jackson, Ph.D.

Reginald purchased a restaurant, a laundry mat and a summer home on the beach. He was the kingpin of a 2.5 million dollar drug operation. Reginald would carry at least three thousand dollars with him every where he went. He loved going to the club and spending money on the girls. Sometimes he would buy drinks for everyone in the club. Reginald and Stacy would have sex with at least two different girls each week.

"Stacy, why don't you call a couple of girls over tonight? I need some."

"You ain't said nothing but a word. Give me a minute and I will get some fly motherfuckers over here."

"You know I like to get my dick sucked, so don't call none of them shady ass bitches."

"Let me handle this, my nigga. I told you I was going to hook you up with some fine motherfuckers."

"Aw right, nigga, she better not be no fat bitch either."

During the winter months, Reginald wore a lot of jewelry and a variety of leather coats. Stacy spent most of his money on cars and motorcycles. Stacy owned a convertible, candy apple red Corvette, a Sedan Deville Cadillac, a Harley Davidson and a Honda touring motorcycle. Reginald never used cocaine, but Stacy snorted some from time to time. Both of the young men would send their mothers large sums of money. Although their mothers weren't happy with what their sons were doing, they never tried to stop them from selling the drugs. Perhaps because their parents were enjoying the money too much.

Reginald's restaurant sold good old fashion soul food. Macaroni and cheese, black-eyed peas, candied yams, ham, barbecue chicken, collard greens, fried catfish, sweet potatoes, fried green tomatoes and more. Reginald would go to Atlanta from time to time looking for old friends so he could impress them with his newfound wealth.

On one late evening in October of 1987, a young man was shot dead in the street. The person that did the shooting was driving a red convertible 325 BMW. Reginald was at home sleeping when there was a knock at the door. He woke up and answered the door.

Wrong Perception

"I'm sorry to wake you, sir, is this your red BMW parked out front?" the policeman asked.

"It sure is. I'm Reginald Maynard, the registered owner, what's the problem officer?"

"I need you to answer a question for me?"

"Okay, fire away?"

"Mr. Maynard, where were you last night?" the policeman asked.

"I was here with my roommate."

"Where is your roommate right now, Mr. Maynard?"

"He's in his room, do you want me to get him for you?"

"If you would."

"I'll be right back."

"Stacy, wake up, man."

"Goddamn Reginald, what's up man?"

"Nigga, get up. There is a policeman at the door."

"Is he on to us?"

"I don't think so, he was just asking where I was last night. Maybe something happened, and he was wondering if I was involved."

"Well, tell that son-of-a-bitch that I'll be out in a few minutes. I need to slip something on."

"All right," Reginald said as he headed back to the front door."

"Hey, he said he will be with you in a minute, officer."

"Okay, I'll be here and I would like to speak with him alone."

"Officer, I am Stacy Mathews, what can I do for you?"

"Is this your red car out here?"

"No, it's my roommate's car."

"Where was your roommate last night?"

"He was here all night."

"How do you know?"

"Because he and I talked until two in the morning and then we fell asleep."

"Could you go and get your roommate for me?"

"Yeah, I'll be right back."

"Yo, Reginald, that motherfucker needs to talk to you again."

"Yes, officer?" Reginald asked.

"I'm going to have to ask you to come with me to the police station."

"What's going on?"

"I'll tell you when we get to the station," the officer said.

The police questioned Reginald, but there was no evidence linking him to the crime. Later that same morning, Reginald was released. Two weeks later, he got a tip from a friend on the police force that the federal marshals had been around asking questions about The Gang. The policeman recommended that Reginald get out of town. Initially, Reginald and Stacy thought that they had too many police officers on their payroll, so there was no reason to leave town. They were still attending college, and the two were making more money in drug sales than they knew what to do with.

One day while doing research in the library, Reginald met a young lady named Michele Greene. Michele actually looked as if she could be his sister. She was a very beautiful girl with a fair complexion and brown curly hair. She and Reginald eventually fell in love. Stacy began dating Michele's younger sister Rhonda. Rhonda was actually more attractive than Michele, but was very immature. Stacy and Reginald appeared to be very happy about the money they were making and the beautiful women in their lives. Reginald purchased another restaurant and another house on the beach where he threw parties every weekend. Stacy and Reginald had concluded that school was no longer important and decided to drop out so that they would have more time for their business.

A week after Reginald dropped out of school, Michele informed him that she was pregnant. Initially, Reginald was ecstatic that he was going to be a father, so he asked Michele to be his wife.

"Michele, will you marry me?"

"No, I told you that my husband is going to be a college graduate."

"Well, you don't seem to have a problem with all of the nice things I buy you."

"So, you better get an education if you want to be my husband. I want a college-educated man and I won't settle for less."

"I never knew you were that serious about me having an education."

"Well, I am. I don't want my child to grow up around drugs," Michele said.

"I will get back into school as soon as I can. I am going to get out of the drug business."

9

Marriage, Lies, and Military

One sunny morning James and Kevin, one of the young men he met at the skating rink, were out riding around in the station wagon and had to stop for gas. Kevin recognized a young lady that he attended high school with by the name of Heather Johnson.

"Hey, man, that girl seems to be waving at you," James said to Kevin, nodding in the direction of Heather.

"Oh, I know her. We went to high school together," Kevin said, waving at Heather to come over.

"Man, you got to introduce me to her," James said as his eyes widened at her beauty.

Heather was every bit of 5'8" and weighed 115 pounds. She could have easily been a model. Heather's complexion was the color of a peach and looked every bit as sweet as one. She had long, dark brown, wavy hair, full sexy lips, high cheekbones and the prettiest baby browns James had ever seen. When Heather walked, she seemed to float on air. She had the grace of a swan when she moved. Kevin and Heather hugged and exchanged hellos before Kevin introduced her to James.

"James, this is my friend Heather Johnson. Heather, this is my partner in crime, James Jones," Kevin said as he stepped out of the way of the vibes between James and Heather.

"Hello James, nice to meet you," Heather said as she extended her hand to him and gave him a big warm smile.

"The pleasure is all mine," James said as he softly gripped Heather's tiny hand.

"So, what are you guys getting into today?" Heather asked as she slowly pulled her hand from James'.

"Well, we thought that we would go to the mall and see what two strong, good looking brothers can get into," Kevin said winking at Heather.

"Well, how would the two of you like to have dinner with two nice young ladies," Heather said as she glanced in James' direction.

"That depends on who the young ladies are," Kevin said, waiting in anticipation.

"Of course me and my roommate, Jamie," Heather said.

"I'm game," James said before Kevin could say anything.

"I guess I'm down too," Kevin said.

"Well, let me pump and pay for my gas and then I'll show you guys where I live," Heather said as she turned to go back to her car.

"I'll pump it for you," James said as he followed behind Heather.

Kevin stood by James' car and watched as James pumped the gas for Heather. Heather stood by the pump and talked to him as he pumped. She asked James if he could pay for the gas for her, since he was parked near the store. James agreed and Heather gave him the seven dollars that it took to fill her car up. While he was in the store paying for the gas, she pulled up along the side of his car and waited for him to come out of the store. Kevin was standing at Heather's car window talking to her when James walked up behind him.

"Okay, follow me, and I'll show you where I live," Heather said as she started her car and waited for James and Kevin to get in their car. James waved to Heather when he was ready. They drove down the road for about a mile before they approached Heather's apartment complex. Heather pulled up in front of building ten, got out of the car and went to James's window and told them that she lived in apartment G. She told them that dinner would be served at 6 P.M. After Heather showed them where she lived, the two men told her that they would be back promptly at six. Kevin and James went to the mall for a few hours and hung out until it was time to go over to Heather's. James went to Rich's department store and sampled some of the cologne so he would smell good when he arrived at Heather's

Wrong Perception

place. The two held true to their word and rung the doorbell promptly at six. Heather answered the door and she had changed into a black spaghetti string, form fitting dress with splits on both sides. James was speechless.

"Hey, guys, I love men who know how to be on time," Heather said holding the door wide open so they could come in. Just then, Jamie appeared from one of the back rooms. Jamie was attractive in her own right, but had nothing on Heather. Jamie was 5'4", weighed about 130 and was a little thick in the hips, but still very shapely. She had a bronze tan complexion. She had short curly hair, thin lips and big green eyes. She had on the exact same dress that Heather did, but in gold which complimented her complexion well. Heather introduced James to Jamie. Kevin already knew Jamie and was still very attracted to her. James and Heather also appeared to be fond of each other.

"You guys have a seat while I put on some music and put the last touches on dinner," Heather said as she walked over to the stereo and turned it to the jazz station. James and Kevin sat on opposite ends of the beige leather sofa while Jamie sat on the matching love seat. Kevin was talking to Jamie when Heather called from the kitchen and asked Jamie to come and help her finish preparing dinner.

"Excuse me, while I go and lend Heather my expertise," Jamie said as she headed to the kitchen. Once Jamie was in the kitchen, James and Kevin gave each other high fives, and little did the guys know, the ladies were in the kitchen doing the same thing. Both Heather and Jamie came out of the kitchen with plates and flatware to set the table. Heather went back in the kitchen for glasses but changed her mind. Heather came to the doorway of the kitchen and asked James and Kevin what they preferred to drink, sweet tea or wine. Heather heard Jamie and Kevin yell, "Wine" and James yell "tea." After a few minutes, Heather came out of the kitchen with two wine glasses and two tall drinking glasses filled with tea. Heather placed the glasses on the table and both she and Jamie stood at the table and called for James and Kevin to come join them. James and Kevin got up from the sofa and stood at the dinner table waiting to be told where to sit. Heather directed James to sit across from her and Kevin sat facing Jamie. While the guys sat down, Jamie and

James D. Jackson, Ph.D.

Heather disappeared into the kitchen. They appeared moments later carrying two plates each of spaghetti and meatballs. After placing the plates down on the table, they went back into the kitchen and brought out tossed salads and garlic bread. James and Kevin waited until Heather and Jamie sat down before digging in. There was little conversation during dinner, but lots of staring. Once they finished dinner, Jamie and Heather invited James and Kevin back into the living room.

Once James and Heather started talking, they realized that they knew many of the same people. James and Heather talked like no one else was in the room. Kevin and Jamie sat on the love seat and were much indulged in their own conversation.

At eleven o'clock, James and Kevin thought it was about time for them to go home. Heather excused her self and went into the kitchen to write her telephone number on a sheet of paper. She went back to where James was sitting and sat beside him.

"Well, come on, man let's go. We've taken up enough of these ladies' time," James said to Kevin.

The four of them stood up to go toward the door, when Heather grabbed James's arm and pulled him back down on the sofa, while Kevin and Jamie continued to head toward the door. Heather slipped James the piece of paper with her telephone number on it and told him to give her a call the next day so the two of them could get together.

All the way home James thought and talked about nothing but Heather. She was very attractive and James could not believe that she was interested in him. He told Kevin how Heather gave him her telephone number, and he asked James if he was going to call her. He told Kevin that he couldn't wait until the next morning so that he could call. After James got home he had a hard time falling asleep because he could not believe how much he liked Heather and how much they had in common. The next morning he waited as long as he could before he called her. At ten o'clock, he called to see if she was awake. When he called, a female answered the telephone.

"Hello, Johnson and Ruffin residence," Heather said.

Wrong Perception

James couldn't tell the difference between Jamie and Heather's voice on the telephone. All James said was hello, and Heather knew immediately who it was.

"James, is that you?" Heather asked.

"Yes, who am I speaking to?" James asked hoping it was Heather.

"It's Heather, crazy," she said, now laughing slightly.

"I really enjoyed myself last night," James said.

"Well, believe me, I enjoyed having you guys over. Especially you," Heather said.

"So what are you going to do today?" James asked.

"Hopefully the same thing you're doing."

"Well, I don't care as long as I see you today," James said now smiling.

"Well, there is something I would like to do," Heather said.

"What's that?"

"Go skating," Heather said with excitement in her voice.

"If that's what you want to do, that's fine with me," James said.

"Well, I'll pick you up tonight at eight," Heather said.

James could not believe that she had made that suggestion because skating was one of his favorite pastimes. He knew that he would make a great impression on her with his skating ability. He gladly accepted her invitation and gave her directions to his house, telling her that he couldn't wait to see her. Heather told him that she would pick him up at 8 P.M.

James laid out a pair of blue jeans and a shirt on the bed and went to cut his hair because he wanted to look his best when Heather arrived to pick him up that evening. At eight o'clock sharp, the doorbell rang and it was Heather. James's mother answered the door.

"Hello, you must be the infamous Heather my son has been talking about nonstop since this morning," Carolyn said as she invited Heather in. "I'm James's mother, Carolyn Jones," she said as she held the door wide open so Heather could come in.

"Nice to meet you, Ms. Jones," Heather said as she came into the house.

At that moment, James came down and asked his mother if she met Heather.

"Yes, I took the liberty of introducing myself," Carolyn said as she smiled at Heather.

"Well, I guess we better be going," James said looking at Heather. He picked up his skates by the door and the two of them were on their way. James couldn't believe how gorgeous Heather looked and everything she said to him went unheard because he was taken by her beauty.

They arrived at the skating rink, and once inside they put on their skates and made their way to the floor. A slow song was playing so they went around the rink a couple of times together. James was hoping that the next song would be a fast one because he wanted to show Heather how talented he was on a pair of skates. The next song was indeed a fast song and one that he liked. James proceeded to skate around the rink very fast, skating forward and backward while spinning around. Heather was so amazed that she stood in the middle of the floor watching with her mouth wide open. After James finished going around the rink a few times, he went back to where Heather was standing with her mouth opened.

"So, how did you like that?" James asked glowing with confidence.

"That was the most amazing skating I have ever seen, you have got to teach me," Heather said, smiling at James.

James agreed to teach Heather how to skate because he knew it would be a way to get closer to her. The two continued to skate and have fun until eleven o'clock. They had a difficult time trying to talk to each other due to the loud music and decided to leave.

Once outside the skating rink, Heather asked James if he wanted to go back to her place so that they could talk and get to know each other better. James asked about her roommate and she told him that her roommate was gone for the evening. At the apartment, the two sat in the living room and Heather put on some soft music. The two of them slow danced with one another, pecking each other on the lips occasionally. Heather became more aggressive and started kissing and licking James on his neck, which drove him wild and made his manhood rise. James's hands started exploring Heather's sleek body over her clothes.

Wrong Perception

Heather slid her hand under James's T-shirt, eased his shirt over his head, and tossed it to the floor. Heather's eyes widened when she saw his big, broad muscular chest. She couldn't help but run her hands over his chest to see if it was real. James pulled Heather's shirt out of her shorts and slowly pulled it over her head and flung it to the floor. He reached behind her back, unsnapped her bra, and flung it to the floor with her shirt. James picked her up, carried her to her bedroom and laid her on the bed. He was lying on top of Heather kissing her when she flipped him over on his back.

"You are one fine man, Mr. Jones," Heather said as she started unbuttoning his pants.

"You ain't so bad yourself, pretty lady."

"Well, let's do this."

"Bring it on," James said as he helped Heather get her shorts and panties off.

"I want to ride you," Heather said as she straddled James, putting the bottom of her feet flat on the bed and squatted down.

"I want you inside of me," Heather said as she put James' manhood inside of her, then interlaced her fingers behind his head and began to slowly move up and down on his manhood.

"Oh, girl, what are you doing to me."

"Does it feel good to you, baby?"

"Yes."

"Huh, baby, does it feel good to you?"

"Oh, hell yeah."

"I'm going to make you love me."

"I think I already do."

"Oh, you ain't seen nothing yet," Heather said as she paused shortly to turn on all the lights in the room.

"What are you going to do now?" James asked.

"I know you want to watch yourself going inside of me," Heather said as she straddled him with her back to him.

"Oh, this feels so good," James said as Heather moved ever so slowly.

"Can you see yourself, going inside of me?" Heather asked.

"Oh, yes," James said as he began to climax.

James was totally blown away. He could not believe that a woman so beautiful could perform so well. James was whipped and in love all at the same time. After the encounter, Heather immediately started talking about nonsexual related things to try and get that innocent, pretty girl image back.

The two began talking about their hobbies and discovered that they had even more in common than they had previously thought. The two talked until 1 A.M. That morning and over the course of the next few weeks the two spent almost every chance they could together. They became very intimate with each other, making love all over the apartment when Jamie was not at home. The two of them talked about how their families had mistreated them and found a connection to each other because of it.

Heather mentioned that her father molested her when she was younger, while James talked about the physical and emotional abuse that he received from his mother. Heather knew that it was getting close to the time for James to return to ASU. She did not want James to leave her so she gave him an ultimatum.

"James, are you looking forward to going back to school?" she asked as she and James watched television in her living room.

"In a way, but I'm going to miss you," James said as he put his arm around her.

"I love you, and I don't want you to leave me. I know if you go you'll forget about me," Heather said as she began to cry.

"Well, what do you expect me to do? I have to get an education," James said as he wiped a tear from her face.

"Marry me before you go back to school," Heather said with excitement in her voice.

"Don't you think we're too young to get married?" James asked.

"You love me don't you?" she asked.

"Yes, I do love you," James said kissing Heather on the lips softly.

"Then marry me," Heather said looking deep into James's eyes.

"I don't know, Heather, that's a big step," James said with a little hesitation in his voice.

"Then are you prepared to end our relationship?" Heather asked with a firm voice.

"What do you mean, end our relationship?" James asked with a confused look on his face.

"James, if you don't marry me it's over between us," Heather said as she got up from the sofa and turned her back to him.

"Heather, I don't want to lose you, you mean the world to me," James said as he got up and hugged her from behind.

"Then let's get married," Heather said as she turned around and faced him.

"Okay, let's do it," he said as he broke out into a smile. James didn't want to lose her because for the first time he felt that he found the one person in the world that really loved him and who gave him the emotional love and support that he had sought from his family. He thought she really understood him and could identify with his pain. Gratified and excited, James went to his mother with what he thought was good news. James and Heather agreed that he should tell his mother the news alone. James was nervous when he approached the door to his mother's house. He took a deep breath before opening the door. When James entered the house, he walked through the living room before he heard Carolyn call from the kitchen.

"I'm in the kitchen, James," Carolyn yelled. She knew it had to be James because he was the only one home at the time. James saw that Carolyn was cooking dinner.

"Hey, Mom, what are you cooking?" he asked, beating around the bush.

"I'm cooking baked chicken breast with wild rice and steamed vegetables," Carolyn said adding more water to the rice.

"Sounds good," James said.

"Well, it should be ready in a little while," Carolyn said taking a seat at the dinner table.

"I'm going to change clothes and I'll be back down for dinner," James said as he slowly walked up the stairs. When he came back downstairs, Carolyn had dinner on the table.

"Mama, I need to talk to you about something," James said as he started putting food in his mouth.

"Well, what is it, son?" Carolyn asked, sitting down to dinner.

"Heather and I have decided to get married," James said.

"You've what!" Carolyn screamed as she jumped up from the table.

"I'm getting married and I want your support," James said.

"Are you out of your damn mind? I'll never support your decision to marry someone you barely know," Carolyn said, yelling to the top of her voice.

"Well, I'm sorry if you can't support me, but I'm going to marry the only person that's shown me love and kindness," James said getting up from the table.

"You don't know a damn thing about this girl or her family. All you know is that this girl has got you pussy whipped," Carolyn said, grabbing James' arm.

"Look, Mama, I just wanted to tell you because I wanted my mother to be happy for me one time in my life," James said snatching his arm from Carolyn's grip.

"Well, I'll never be happy about my son ruining his life for a piece of tail," Carolyn snapped.

"Sorry you feel that way, but I should have expected this from you. You never gave a damn about my happiness," James said as he walked out the door.

"You're making the biggest mistake of your life, and I'll have nothing to do with it" Carolyn yelled as James got in his station wagon and drove away. James stayed the night with Heather and the next day he went to Carolyn's while she was at work to pack his belongings. He went back to Heather's after packing because he had no other place to go. He felt disowned by his mother.

Since James already felt that he had no support from his family in anything else he wanted to do, he decided to marry the one person who did show him love and support. On August 21, 1987 James and Heather went down to the courthouse and were pronounced man and wife.

James was very content about being married to Heather. He had plans of starting a family immediately because he wanted a family that he could love that would also love him. Heather was very excited about her decision to marry James. She told her family how much she loved him and that they would be trying to have children soon. Although Heather was only eighteen years old, she was unbelievable in the bedroom. James was not that adept with sex, so she had him "whipped" pretty bad. James thought that he would really enjoy being married to Heather for the rest of his life.

After getting married, James returned to ASU. Due to all of his studying during the summer, he was able to finally test out of developmental studies and start taking normal college courses. When he returned, he realized that he missed his wife too much to allow her to live in Atlanta while he lived on campus. He told Heather that he was going to bring her back with him the next time he came to Atlanta. Once James presented his marriage license to the school administration, he was no longer eligible to live in the single student dormitory and had to move into married student housing. James had to turn in his meal card and was trying to sustain himself and his new wife with any food that they could scrounge up. James could not afford to attend ASU any longer. His family could not afford to give him any financial support and James could not find a job anywhere. James and Heather discussed their future and decided that they would both enlist in the Army together. The two took the Armed Services Vocational Aptitude Battery (ASVAB) and waited for the test results. While James was on break from class, he stopped by the apartment to see if the recruiter had called with their test results. Heather was in the bed watching the small black and white television when she heard the door open.

"James," Heather called out, waiting for a response.

"Yeah, has the recruiter called with the results?" James asked.

"No, not yet," Heather said as she got out of the bed and went into the kitchen where James was.

"What's there here to eat?" James said looking in the cabinets.

"I've made some chicken salad," Heather said.

"Well, could you make me a sandwich, please," James said as he sat on the stool at the counter. Heather made James's sandwich and gave it to him with a glass of cherry Kool-Aid. Just as James bit into his sandwich, the telephone rang.

"Hello, Jones residence," Heather said.

James D. Jackson, Ph.D.

"Yes, is James Jones in? This is Staff Sergeant (SSG) Thomas, I'm calling about the test results."

"Great, we've been waiting on your call, hold on," Heather said as she handed James the telephone.

"Hello, this is James Jones."

"Hello, Mr. Jones, this is SSG Thomas and I have you and your wife's test results."

"Well, how did we do?" James asked clearing his throat.

"Congratulations, you and your wife passed. Now the only thing we need is for you and your wife to bring in your high school diplomas, social security cards and birth certificates as soon as possible," the recruiter said.

"Well, we'll be down first thing in the morning," James said, hanging up the telephone and letting out a yell.

"What happened, what did he say?" Heather asked.

"We both passed. Now all we have to do is take him our diplomas, birth certificates and social security cards," James said as he picked Heather up and swung her around. "Our troubles are over. Come on, let's go find our information," James said, forgetting about his hunger.

"James, I need to talk to you," Heather said.

"We don't have time to talk. We need to find this stuff first," James said as he headed to the bedroom.

"James, I don't have a high school diploma!" Heather yelled out.

"What in the hell did you just say?" James asked as he came back into the kitchen.

"I don't have my high school diploma. I lied to you because I knew a college man wouldn't date or marry a high school dropout," Heather said trying to hug James.

"I can't believe what I'm hearing. Get the fuck away from me!" James screamed as he took his fist and punched the wall, making a hole in it.

"James, I'm sorry, but I didn't want to lose the best thing that has ever happened to me," Heather said as tears flowed down her face.

"What else have you lied to me about? Come clean now and maybe we can get on with our lives," James said staring at Heather.

"I haven't lied to you about anything else, I swear," Heather said reaching out to James.

"Look, I need some time to think about what I'm going to do. You have put me in a tough situation," James said walking out the door.

"James!" Heather yelled.

It was three hours before James came back to the apartment. When he opened the door, Heather was sitting on the sofa with all of the lights out.

"James, I'm sorry for lying to you," Heather said. James turned on the light before saying anything. Once the lights were on, James could see that Heather had been crying. He went over and sat next to her on the sofa.

"Come here, we need to talk," James said as he reached out to Heather. Heather fell into James's strong arms and cried.

"James, I promise that I will never lie to you again," Heather said sobbing.

"I've thought about it and I have no choice but to go into the military without you," James said.

"James, again I am sorry and I'll make it up to you somehow," Heather said hugging James tight around his neck.

James withdrew from college a week later and enlisted in the United States Army. He knew that a private in the Army did not make a lot of money, but he was counting on the two of them going into the Army because with both of them making money, they would be all right. James enlisted in the Army, helped Heather earn her GED and paid for her to begin taking college courses.

James entered the Army on December 31, 1987 and attended basic training at Fort Jackson, South Carolina. Due to his superb physical condition, the Army physical fitness program was very easy for him to adapt to and excel in. Although James's mother was not happy with the fact that Heather and James were married, she agreed to allow Heather to live with her while James was away. Carolyn told Heather that it was okay for her to live there until James found a place for the two of them. While at

James D. Jackson, Ph.D.

Fort Jackson, James would call Heather from time to time, to see how she was doing. The third time James called Heather she told him that she was pregnant and expecting in August of 1988. James was very excited about being a father, but he knew that Heather could never join the military now without giving up custody of their child. James wanted to receive a lot of commendation at graduation so he would stay up at night when the other soldiers were in the bed, doing push-ups and sit-ups because he knew what he needed to do to get into excellent physical condition. James conditioned his body so well that he was the most physically fit soldier in the company.

"Someone get me Private Jones," Drill Sergeant Moore said.

"Yes, Drill Sergeant, were you looking for me?"

"Yes, I was, Private Jones. I have noticed that you are the most physically fit soldier in the company. Is that a fair assessment?"

"Well, I did score the highest score on the last physical fitness test."

"I intend on sending you to the soldier of the cycle board. This board will ask you questions on military knowledge, current events and the chain of command. I really believe that when your record here goes before the board, you will win. This board meets tomorrow, so you have the rest of the day to prepare."

"Thanks a lot, Drill Sergeant."

At the soldier of the cycle board, James answered more questions correctly than any other soldier that was selected to attend the board. He was named the outstanding soldier of the cycle. James's mother, sister, grandmother and wife attended the basic training graduation. James' mother was overwhelmed with pride when she saw her son being presented with his awards for a high physical fitness score, high marksmanship, and the outstanding soldier of the cycle. After the graduation, James got a chance to spend the rest of the day with his family.

"James, I am so proud of you," Heather said.

"Well, thanks, baby, I am happy that basic training is over. That was one of the hardest things I have ever done."

"Well, it's over now, and you did a good job."

Wrong Perception

James thanked his family for coming to his graduation. The following day he boarded a plane headed to Fort Sill, Oklahoma, the home of the Army's artillery school. There he would receive his Advanced Individual Training (AIT). James was headed to Fort Sill to learn to be a fire support specialist. While at Fort Sill James learned his craft and excelled in the physical fitness program offered there.

James graduated from the artillery school in March of 1988. He had military orders for Fort Stewart in Hinesville, Georgia, which was forty miles west of Savannah, Georgia. James arrived at Fort Stewart in April of 1988. He was assigned to Headquarters Company, 2nd Battalion, 35th Field Artillery. He was promoted to Private First Class and happy to be finished with Basic and Advanced Individual Training. He was reunited with his wife, and they were waiting eagerly for the arrival of their child. It was rough for James for the first couple of years because a private First Class in the Army does not make very much money. He had to care for his family by providing a clean apartment in a nice neighborhood, food and clothing. In June of 1988, James's maternal grandfather died of lung cancer. James was devastated by the loss of his grandfather. He would often go by and spend time with his grandfather. Many people that knew James's grandfather would always comment on how much James looked like him. Since James's grandfather did not have a lot of education, he was not so concerned about who were his smart grandchildren, he was just happy to be a grandfather. That was probably why James felt that he had a real connection with him.

On August 12, 1988, Heather gave birth to their first child, Beverly Jones. She was born at 8 P.M. At first, Beverly seemed to be a normal, healthy baby, but after ten hours of being alive, she took a turn for the worse.

"Hello, Mr. Jones this is the head nurse from Doctors Hospital."

"Yes, is there something wrong?" James asked, now coming out of his sleep.

"Yes, Mr. Jones you need to come to the hospital immediately," the nurse said.

"What's going on?" James said, getting concerned.

"There is a problem with your daughter. Mr. Jones, you need to come quickly," the nurse said with urgency in her voice.

"I'm on my way," James said hanging up the telephone without saying good-bye.

James was driving like a New York taxi driver through the bare streets. When he arrived at the hospital, the elevators were taking too long so James ran up seven flights of stairs. When he reached the nurses' station, he was not even breathing hard.

"I'm Mr. Jones, how's my baby, where is she?" James asked.

"Mr. Jones, I'm Nurse Flowers, I was the one that called you. Let me call Dr. Edwards, he wants to talk to you and Mrs. Jones," Nurse Flowers said, picking up the telephone.

It wasn't a full minute before Dr. Edwards was out at the nurses' station and whisking James to Heather's room to talk to them both. When Heather saw James, she broke out in tears immediately.

"James, they won't tell me what's wrong with our baby. Have they told you what's wrong with her?" Heather said with tears streaming down her face.

"I just got here and they haven't told me anything yet," James said as he went over and sat on the bed next to Heather.

"Mr. and Mrs. Jones, I wanted to talk to the both of you at the same time," Dr. Edwards said opening Beverly's chart.

"Doctor, what's wrong with our little girl?" James asked, holding Heather's hand.

"We are getting her prepared to be flown to a more equipped hospital in Savannah. Your daughter has been diagnosed with beta strep ducoccus," Dr. Edwards said with sadness in his eyes.

"What is that and will she be all right?" James asked with fear in his voice.

"I'm sorry to have to be the one to tell you but the disease is fatal," Dr. Edwards said as tears formed in his eyes.

"Well, how did she get it?" James questioned as he held Heather tighter and the both of them broke down and cried.

"It's found mostly in newborns and we don't know how to treat it, but at a more equipped hospital they would be able to sustain her life longer," Dr. Edwards said. Heather started to cry and scream uncontrollably. Dr. Edwards called for the nurse to sedate Heather. James helped to hold Heather while the nurse gave her the shot. Heather was out almost immediately. James gently wiped the tears from her face and softly kissed her lips. He went to the nursery and watched as his beautiful little girl was being hooked up to all kinds of machines and receiving oxygen. James felt helpless standing there with tears flowing freely from his now red eyes. When Beverly was ready to go, James asked if he could go with them on the helicopter ride to Savannah. He was told that there wasn't enough room, because the staff would need the room to work on Beverly. The staff rushed by James so fast he didn't even get a chance to see her tiny little face. They left him standing in the corridor alone. James could see the staff load the equipment and Beverly onto the helicopter and fly away. James went back to Heather's room and waited to hear any information about his daughter. Heather was unconscious so James sat by the window and stared up at the moon and stars that lit the sky and prayed.

En route to the hospital in Savannah, Beverly died. After James had been staring out the window praying for thirty minutes, Dr. Edwards walked into Heather's room.

"Mr. Jones, I'm sorry, your baby passed away on the way to the hospital," Dr. Edwards said, lowering his head. James said nothing as he sunk deeper into the chair and cried.

"Mr. Jones, is there anything I or the nurses can do for you?" Dr. Edwards asked.

"Yes, you can, bring my baby back," James said angrily. Dr. Edwards said nothing and left the room.

James and his wife were devastated by the loss of their first born. James could not understand why God had taken away his beautiful daughter. He refused to go to work for two weeks after the death of his daughter. Many of James and Heather's family attended the funeral in Atlanta. Beverly was buried next to James's maternal grandfather, James B. Lawton. He was so hurt by the death of his daughter that he wanted to die himself. Shortly after the death of his daughter, James was promoted to specialist, E-4.

James and Heather's marriage was deteriorating. Heather was making James's life a living hell after the death of their daughter. She would always accuse James of cheating on her whenever he came home late from work. James would always explain to her that his First Sergeant would decide to talk to the company longer on some occasions. Heather would act very immature. She would lock James out of the house and talk to him through the window whenever he came home late. Sometimes it would be hours before she opened the door. James would always tell his wife that he loved her and that she could call his job if she thought he was lying. James tried to be more attentive to Heather's needs, but he was hurting from the death of their daughter also. Heather didn't care about James's pain, only her own. James suggested to Heather that they have another baby. It had been two months since Beverly passed away, and James wanted his marriage to work. The doctors told James and Heather that they could try to have another baby after six months, but James felt that they wouldn't make it if they kept going the way they were going.

"Heather, I know it's only been a short time, but I would like for us to try at having another baby," James said as he was getting undressed to get in bed.

"I don't know, James, the doctor said for us to wait a least six months," Heather said and she put on her nightgown.

"Look, Heather, something has to change. If we don't make a change, this marriage will not last," James said getting in bed. Heather said nothing. She got in the bed and started kissing James. She would do anything to keep her husband. This was the first time that James and Heather had made love since the death of their daughter. The next month James and Heather found out that she was pregnant. This time they took every precaution to have a healthy baby.

In August of 1989, Heather gave birth to their second child, Janet Nicole Jones. Janet was born a very healthy baby girl. James was so happy about having a child that for the first six weeks of Janet's life, he washed and changed her whenever she needed changing and refused to allow anyone else, including Heather, to do it when he came home from work. When James would get home from work and needed to go to the store for something, he would always take his baby with him. James would try to read a story to Janet every night before he put her to bed.

Wrong Perception

On January 5, 1990, James decided to call his mother's house to see how everyone in the family was doing. When Jeff answered the telephone, James was shocked to hear his voice.

"What are you doing home?"

James asked Jeff what he was doing there and why he wasn't in school. While in his sophomore year at the University of Staton, Jeff did not maintain the mandatory 2.0 GPA and was expelled. Jeff's parents had big dreams for his future because he was considered a gifted child in elementary school. Jeff went on to explain to James that he wasn't doing as well as everyone thought he was doing in school. He was caught up in all of the excitement of being away from home and being on his own.

Jeff also told James about the car trouble he was having. He asked Jeff what his mother thought about his most recent disappointment. Jeff explained that he had just gotten home and hadn't spoken to their mother about it yet. He wasn't looking forward to the encounter because he knew that this news would hurt his mother deeply. James, who always thought of himself as a father figure to Jeff, thought of a solution to Jeff's problem. James thought that he could pay Jeff back for all the abuse he put him through when he was a child. James told Jeff that he would help him get back on his feet if he wanted to come and live with him and his family in Fort Stewart, Georgia. He promised to get Jeff's car fixed and put him back in school to get his grades back up to standard. Jeff jumped at the opportunity to get away from what he knew was going to be an uncomfortable situation with his mother. Jeff decided that he would leave the following Friday and head for Fort Stewart. It was just then that Carolyn came through the door and was surprised to see Jeff home. Jeff told his mother that James was on the telephone and to let him know when she was finished talking to James because he needed to speak to her.

James didn't tell his mother about the plans that he and Jeff made, he left that for Jeff to do. Once Carolyn was off the telephone, she started interrogating Jeff about why he was home during the middle of a school week. Jeff knew he had to tell his mother the bad news. When he told his mother what had happened to him at school, Carolyn hit the roof. She was very upset with Jeff, while letting him know how disappointed she was in him. Jeff explained to his mother that he would be leaving soon to go and live with his brother.

When Jeff arrived at James's house, James did exactly what he told him he would do. First, he fixed Jeff's car. Secondly, he enrolled Jeff in two college courses on post that Jeff completed, making two A's. Thirdly, he never asked Jeff for one dime for food or rent, while Jeff lived with him. After living with James for three months, one day while Jeff was working out in the weight room at Fort Stewart, he met a German girl named Tanya Taylor. She was recently divorced from a soldier stationed at Fort Stewart. Jeff thought that Tanya was very pretty so he asked her for her telephone number. After their first telephone conversation, Jeff and Tanya started dating. In March, Jeff and Tanya decided that they wanted to live together. The couple moved to Savannah and began their lives together. After working a few odd-end jobs, Jeff got a job working as a car salesman with a new car dealership.

Over the next year, James was able to complete his associate of arts degree in night school, while gaining popularity among the soldiers at Fort Stewart because of his athletic ability. He led his company softball team with sixteen homeruns, his flag football team in touchdowns and was named the post one-hundred-meter champion in 1989 and 1990. In June of 1990, James and Heather found out that Heather was pregnant with their third child.

10

Desert Shield / Desert Storm

In August of 1990, Iraq invaded Kuwait. Fort Stewart, at that time, was the home of the mighty 24th Infantry Division, which was considered one of the best desert-trained divisions in the world. On August 2, 1990, while James was attending the promotion board to become a Sergeant E-5, Fort Stewart was placed on alert for Operation Desert Shield. Fort Stewart was one of the first divisions to arrive in Saudi Arabia and prepared to go to war with Iraq. James arrived in Saudi Arabia on the 26th of August. He called Heather when he reached the desert.

"Hello?" Heather said when she answered the telephone.

"Heather, it's me, James."

"Well, I see you made it there all right," Heather said.

"Yeah, we got here about three hours ago."

"What's it like over there?" she asked.

"It's hot as hell over here. The temperature is about 115 degrees with very little wind."

"Well, do you have any water to drink?"

"Yeah, we got two bottles per person, issued to us when we got off the plane."

"How long was the flight?" Heather asked.

"It was about eighteen hours, including the stopover in Germany."

"What do the people look like over there?" Heather questioned.

"They look like Blacks and Hispanics."

"Well, did they say something to you when you got off the plane?"

"No, but they smiled and pointed at me. The interpreter with us informed me that they said I look like one of them."

"Well, you know what they say, light skinned blacks can fit in anywhere."

"Yeah, I guess I see what they mean," James replied. "I have been told that we will be receiving 'hazardous duty pay' while we are over here. I think this will be a good chance for us to save money."

"I agree," Heather said as she cleared her throat.

"I want you to go to the commissary whenever you need food and minimize your trips to fast food restaurants," James said.

"I will do just that. I will save as much money as I can."

"Who knows, we might win this war, and I will come home a war hero."

"Yeah, I just hope you come home alive and in one piece," Heather said. "Once you get an address, send it to me so I can send you care packages. I will be sure to send you plenty of Gatorade."

"Okay, as soon as I get an address, I will call and let you know," James said.

"I am going to try to write you everyday," Heather promised as she told James that she had to go because Janet was crying.

James was assigned as a member of the 4th Battalion 64th Armor Regiment. He served as a member of the fire support element located at the battalion's tactical operation center. When all of the vehicles and equipment made it over to Saudi Arabia, the 24th Infantry Division started preparing for one of the most successful wars in U.S. history. James's daily duties included fire support planning, and burning the human urine and feces that accumulated in the outhouse pales. On November 1, 1990 James was promoted to Sergeant and did not have to dispose of human waste anymore. That job was only given to soldiers E-4 and below. After being promoted to Sergeant, James was assigned to D Company, 4-64 Armor. He was given his own fire support team vehicle (FIST-V) to provide the indirect fire support for the company. One evening when Private Jones, the company commander's driver, was handing out mail, a letter was addressed to any service member from the state of Georgia.

Wrong Perception

"Sergeant Jones, I know you are from Georgia, so I wondered if you wanted to respond to this letter?" Private Jones asked.

"Well, who is the letter from?"

"I'm not sure, but it's addressed to any service member from Georgia."

"Give it to me, I'll read it."

When James opened the letter, there was a picture of the young girl. The young girl's name was Lisa Walker. She had red hair, freckles on her face and was a student in the third grade. James responded to the letter. He and the young girl wrote about three or four more letters to each other during the time that James was in the Gulf.

"Oh, by the way, Sergeant Jones, the commander wants to have a meeting it ten minutes and he wants you and your lieutenant to be there," the commander's driver said.

"Okay, I will let my lieutenant know."

James walked around to the other side of the FIST-V where his lieutenant was. "Lieutenant, the commander is having a meeting in ten minutes and he wants us there."

"All right, let me get my notebook," Lieutenant Gresham said.

"Okay, I'll be waiting for you on the other side of the vehicle."

"All right."

Captain Keith Logan was the company commander for D Company. "Listen up, guys. We should have our mission in a few days. We need to start getting ready for war with Iraq."

The 24th was lead by Major General Barry McCaffrey. Only after a few short weeks of preparation, the 24th was ready for war. The 24th was standing by, waiting on the orders from the President of the United States. President Bush spent a few days during the Thanksgiving holiday with the troops and informed them that they would not be going home until the war was over. Many of the soldiers shouted out to the president when he made the comment, "Then let's get this war started so we can go home." On January 17, 1991, while listening to the radio in Saudi Arabia, a news flash interrupted the airways. The message was loud and clear. "The war with Iraq has begun."

James D. Jackson, Ph.D.

The battalion commander, LTC Duane Grier of 4-64 Armor Battalion, gathered all of his company commanders and briefed them on the situation.

"Gentlemen, today is January 20, 1991. The war in the Gulf has begun. Allied air and naval forces began the destruction of essential Iraqi strategic, operational, and tactical targets."

"Sir, what do you want us to do tonight?" Captain Keith Logan asked.

"Nothing today. Get a good night's sleep and I will see all of you back here, not tomorrow, but the following morning at eight. I'll talk to you in great detail about our plan of attack."

By the end of the second day, the coalition air component had achieved air superiority. By January 21st, the Iraqi Air Force was incapable of operations. Air operations continued to strike at essential systems in the heart of Iraq as well as at the Republican Guard and front-line Iraqi forces. Special forces units out of Fort Bragg were operating throughout the theater.

The coalition set the final conditions for the ground attack. It moved the VII Corps by ground tactical movement and the XVIII Airborne Corps by road convoy from defensive positions in the east to attack positions up to five hundred miles away, west of Kuwait. As air interdiction and operational deception operations continued, allied ground forces were set to execute the decisive action against the enemy.

The major ground operation began in the early morning hours on the 24th of February. The objective was to drive Iraqi forces from Kuwait, requiring defeat of the Republican Guard divisions in southern Iraq. The plan for achieving this, entailed a deliberate attack along the Kuwaiti/Saudi Arabia border by the 1st Marine Expeditionary Force and Arab coalition forces. Included in the plan were deception operations to fix Iraqi forces while the VII Corps and XVIII Airborne Corps swept around to the west of the Iraqi defenses to envelop them. The intent of the strike was to strike deep into Iraq to sever Iraqi lines of communications and to isolate and defeat the elite Republican Guard. The coalition forces were successful in meeting their objective.

Wrong Perception

Based on the initial success, United States Central Command (USCENTCOM) began the coalition's main effort fourteen hours early. The XVIII Airborne Corps continued to attack west of the Iraqi obstacle belt with the 24th Infantry Division and the 3rd Armored Cavalry Regiment (ACR) to seize objectives inside Iraq. By the evening of February 26th, the VII Corps had turned ninety degrees to the east, fixed the Republican Guard and opened a corridor for the XVIII Airborne Corps to continue their attack to the east after having secured the coalition's west flank. The 24th Infantry Division had reached the Euphrates River, blocked Iraqi western routes of withdrawal and turned east with the 3rd ACR to engage the Republican Guard. Throughout the theater of operations, coalition forces held the initiative. Coalition forces attacked on the night of February 26th, with VII Corps making the main attack against three Republican Guard Armored Divisions and parts of the other Iraqi formations, including the Jihad Corps. In the south of the corps sector, the 1st Infantry Division conducted a night passage of lines through the engaged 2nd ACR and immediately made contact. To their north, the 1st and 3rd Armored Divisions pressed the attack east while the 1st Cavalry Division, released from USCENTCOM reserve, moved almost two hundred kilometers in twenty-four hours to an attack position. XVIII Airborne Corps pressed the attacks east to the north of VII Corps with attack aviation of the 101st Airborne Division, ground and air attacks of the 3rd ACR and 24th Infantry Division. The allied pressed the attack relentlessly through the night and during the day of the 27th of February toward the Iraqi City of Basrah and the coast of Kuwait.

Nearing the conclusion of the ground attack, the mighty 24th witnessed a not-so-pretty site. James personally witnessed the total destruction of twenty-five Iraqi tanks and approximately seventy-eight dead Iraqi soldiers arrayed across the desert floor. Some of the bodies were charred from the fires inside the vehicles and dead enemy dismounts were scattered along the desert floor with multiple holes in their bodies from machine gun fire. As the fire support sergeant, James was responsible for requesting artillery or mortar fires on targets greater than six hundred meters. His additional responsibility was to dismount from his fire support team vehicle and collect all of the rifles lying in the open or next to a dead Iraqi soldier. James personally collected twenty-seven AK47's, maps and other types of Iraqi equipment. The company that he was assigned to captured forty-eight Iraqi soldiers. By the morning of February 28th, the Republican Guard divisions were effectively routed and incapable of further coordinated resistance.

At 0800 hours on the 28th of February, after the coalition achieved the military objectives of the operation, President Bush called for coalition forces to cease offensive operations.

When the war was over, James called home to tell his wife and learned that she had given birth to a little girl. Three weeks after the war was over, the soldiers of the mighty 24th were airborne en route to the United States. On the plane ride home, James was talking to Lieutenant Byron Gresham.

"Lieutenant, I am so happy to be going home to see my family."

"Yeah, I know what you mean," Lieutenant Gresham said. "I married my wife two weeks before we came over here, so you know I am ready to see her again."

"My wife told me that she has saved a lot of money during my time in the Gulf," James said.

"My wife better be ready, because this build up is going to be released on her," James said laughingly.

"Yeah, I know what you mean," Lieutenant Gresham said. "I am horny as hell. I can't wait to get home and make love to my wife."

James and the rest of the soldiers of the 24th were greeted with a hero's welcome once they reached the airport in Savannah and again at home at Fort Stewart. When the bus arrived at Fort Stewart, the commanders formed up their companies as they marched toward the hundreds of family and friends waiting on the opposite side of field. James was greeted by his mother, sister, grandmother, Johnny, Heather, and his daughter Janet and newborn daughter Tammy, who was three weeks old.

"Hey, baby," Heather said with tears in her eyes.

"Hey, everybody," James said as he hugged his wife and reached for his daughter Janet.

Wrong Perception

Janet ran from her father and into her uncle's arms. She did not recognize the man who had given her life. Luckily, the chaplains had prepared the soldiers for this, so it wasn't that hard for James to accept and understand. James then picked up his newborn who was lying in a baby carrier and hugged the rest of his family members.

James immediately signed out on leave for twenty days to spend time with his family in Atlanta. Before he drove to Atlanta, he asked Heather how much money she saved while he was away. Heather told him that she was not able to save any money because she did not feel like cooking when she was pregnant. She told James that she ate at a restaurant practically everyday while he was away. He was very angry with Heather because she had been telling him when he called that she was saving a lot of money. He really felt like a fool when he remembered bragging to the other soldiers in his unit about how much money his wife saved while he was away.

When James got to Atlanta there was a welcome home party waiting for him. During his tour of duty in Saudi Arabia, Lisa Walker wrote her address and telephone number on the last letter she mailed to Sergeant Jones. The young girl's address placed her within fifteen minutes from his house in Atlanta. James called the young girl's parents and informed them that he was in town. The family prepared dinner and invited Sergeant Jones over. He decided to wear his green Army uniform to remove all doubt to who he was. It was definitely a proud moment for Sergeant Jones once he reached the house. The young girl also sent pictures of the family over to Saudi Arabia, so it was very easy for James to identify the family members among the many friends that were stopping by to meet him.

"So tell us, Sergeant Jones, are you happy to be home?" Mr. Walker said as he shook James's hand.

"I am very happy to be home," James said as he began introducing Heather to the rest of the family.

"Well, I hope you like chicken because I have prepared chicken for you," Mrs. Walker said.

"That's fine. I've been eating food out of a plastic bag for the last eight months, anything would be good right about now," James said as the family laughed. They enjoyed a wonderful chicken dinner and asked James plenty of questions about the war.

"Were you scared over there?" Mr. Walker asked.

"No doubt about it," James responded. "I am happy that I made it back in one piece and am able to have dinner with you fine people."

"Well, it is our pleasure having you in our home, and you and your wife are always welcome," Mr. Walker said.

"James, I told a lot of my classmates that you were coming over here, and they asked me if you could come to my school and talk to them about the war," Lisa said.

"If I have time, I most certainly will," James said.

"I would really appreciate it if you could do that for my daughter," Mrs. Walker said.

"I'll do my best. Where is the school?" James asked.

"It's right around the corner from here. Come with me real quick so I can show you," Mr. Walker said.

After Mr. Walker showed James where the school was, James responded optimistically. "All right, I will make sure I stop in tomorrow and talk to the students.

"Thanks again, Sergeant, you don't know how much this means to Lisa and our family," Mr. Walker said as James followed him back to the house.

"I have really enjoyed the home cooked meal," James said. "I need to make my rounds now because I will be heading back to Fort Stewart in a couple of days," he said as he headed out the door and got into his car to go to Heather's grandmother's house.

"I really enjoyed myself at the Walkers' house today," James said. "It feels good to know that Americans really respect soldiers."

"I could tell how happy you were, I am proud of you baby," Heather said.

"I think I'm going to be in the Army for a long time. I'm proud to be an American soldier," James said.

Once the couple reached Heather's grandmother's house, James was greeted with another hero's welcome home.

Wrong Perception

"There he is, our proud Army soldier," Heather's grandmother said as she hugged James when he entered the house.

"I am so happy to be back," James said.

"I have made you a cake and bought some ice cream," Heather's mother said, as she too was there to greet James.

There were about ten of Heather's relatives there to greet James on this Saturday evening. He made his way around the room to greet them all. Heather had two younger cousins that attended the same elementary school. Felix was in the third grade and Sheila was in the fifth grade.

"James, could you please come to our school and talk to the students in my class?" Felix and Sheila asked.

"Sure, when do you want me to come?" James asked.

"We will ask our teachers on Monday when you can come, and we will let you know," Felix said.

"Okay, just let me know," James said.

When Heather's cousins returned home after school on Monday, they both called James and told him that their teachers said that it would be okay if he came on Wednesday.

While at the elementary school, James really enjoyed himself talking about the war. The children thought that it was very funny when James told them that he had to dig a hole in the ground to use the restroom.

"Are you a general?" one of the students asked as James was dressed in his dress green Army uniform.

"No, I am a sergeant," James responded.

"Like Sergeant Carter on Gomer Pile," one of the students said as the other students laughed.

"Yes, just like Sergeant Carter on the Gomer Pile show," James responded.

"Sergeant Jones, how did you feel when you saw blood and dead bodies?" one student asked.

"It was very tough at first, because I hate to see anyone in pain or dead. I must admit though, it was better to see dead Iraqi's than to see dead Americans," James said.

"Sergeant Jones, can I have your autograph?" one of the students asked.

"Sure, if you really want it," James replied. All of the students in the class lined up to get Sergeant Jones's autograph.

After James finished talking to Sheila's class, he made all of his rounds talking to old friends and family before returning to Fort Stewart. The soldiers were told to continue to wear their desert fatigues around town for the first month back from Saudi Arabia, because all of the stores in Hinesville wanted to welcome their soldiers home.

11

Gaining Confidence

James was thrilled about all the respect he was getting. He never imagined in his wildest dreams that he would be a sergeant and a war veteran.

According to Army regulation, soldiers normally attend the Primary Leadership Development Course (PLDC), prior to pinning on their sergeant stripes. The only time that a soldier can be promoted to sergeant without PLDC is if they are in a war zone at the time of their eligibility. The one stipulation to the war zone promotion is that the newly promoted sergeant must attend and graduate from PLDC upon sixty days after they have returned home from the war.

"Sergeant Jones, you need to get your stuff together to attend PLDC," First Sergeant Oliver said. "Now, you know you must pass the course if you want to continue to be a sergeant."

"I know. My platoon sergeant has been telling me the same thing. Is PLDC really that hard?" James asked.

"I would not say that it's hard, but it damn sure ain't easy. I have seen plenty of soldiers get sent back to their units, so you better go there with your head on straight."

"First Sergeant, I won't let you or my family down. I am proud of being a sergeant and serving my country. I'll graduate, don't worry."

"I sure hope so, because I would hate to have to pull those chevrons off of your collar."

At PLDC James learned a great deal about military leadership, but more importantly, he learned a lot about himself. Graduating 8th in his class of 122 students gave him the confidence to believe in his intellectual ability, rather than believe that he had some sort of learning disability.

"Heather, I am so happy that it is finally over. The first sergeant had me kind of worried about this course," James said.

"I always knew you could do it," Heather said.

James graduated with honors and his wife and close coworkers were there to congratulate him. One month later he was approached by one of the field artillery captains, Captain Daniel McDonald.

"Sergeant Jones, why are you standing outside of the reenlistment office?" Captain McDonald asked.

"I am thinking about reenlisting for a couple of more years."

"Have you ever considered becoming a commissioned officer?"

"I seriously thought about it, but all the schools that I was able to contact were not accepting any more incoming cadets for the year. The schools informed me that during the time that I was in Saudi Arabia the slots were filled and that I needed to apply the following year."

"Do you really want to be an officer?"

"Yes sir."

"Follow me to my office, I think I have a school for you."

Captain McDonald had some information about a college that was still looking for cadets. Augusta College in Augusta, Georgia was looking for students with prior military experience and at least two years of college. Captain McDonald gave James the phone number and he called the school.

"This is Captain Watson, how may I help you?"

"I am Sergeant James Jones and I am looking at a flyer that says you are looking for cadets."

"Yes, we are, where are you calling from?"

"I'm calling from Fort Stewart, Georgia."

"School starts in a couple of weeks, will you be able to separate from the Army in time?"

"I sure hope so. I recently returned from Desert Storm and am eager to start school and pursue a commission."

"So you are a Desert Storm veteran."

"Yes ma'am, I am."

"Well, if you enter our program, you will be the first Desert Storm veteran to do so. When can you come to the college to see if we are what you are looking for?"

"Hold on a minute. Captain McDonald, the captain on the other line wants to know when I can come up there."

"Well, tomorrow is Friday, so I will sign a three day pass and you can go up there tomorrow and stay the weekend if you want to."

"I can come up there tomorrow," James said as he got back on the telephone.

"We are only looking for applicants with two years of college and prior military experience. I know you have the military experience, but how about the education?"

"I have completed my associate's degree in night school, so, yes ma'am, I'm qualified."

"Okay, sounds good, we will see you tomorrow," Captain Watson said as the two said their good-byes.

James applied to Augusta College and was accepted into the college and the Reserve Officer Training Corps (ROTC) program. During the time that Heather was at Fort Stewart, James paid for her to take the GED, enroll in one year of college courses, obtain nursing assistance certification and attend a medical coding class.

James told Heather that she would need to find a job the moment they reached Augusta because he was going to have to buckle down and make good grades to ensure that he would be selected for active duty. He knew that working while going to school was not a good idea if he was trying to maintain a grade point average above a 3.0, considering his background.

"I was never a good student, so I'm really going to need your help to keep my grades up."

"I'm here for you now. We will make it through these trying times together," Heather said.

James told Heather that if she could manage to hold on to a job for the two years, while he was in school, she would never have to work another day in her life. James was officially released from active duty on September 13, 1991. James would be attending Augusta College where he would be pursuing his degree in sociology, and seeking his commission as a second lieutenant in the U.S. Army.

Back in South Carolina, Reginald was back in school and flirting with graduating and marrying Michele. He would take Michele anywhere she wanted to go, and would buy her anything that she wanted. Reginald bought her expensive clothes and jewelry. He became her sugar daddy.

"Michele, let's go shopping today. I saw an outfit that I think would look good on you."

"Okay, sweetie, if you want to take me shopping, then I want to go."

"I also want you to pick the restaurant where we are going to eat lunch."

"Okay, I can do that."

"If you see anything that you want, just let me know and I will buy it for you."

Reginald was head over heels in love with this woman and he did not care who knew it. Reginald wanted this lady to be his wife and there was not even another woman that he called occasionally. Michele had it all. She stood about 5'5 and weighed about 115 pounds. She was "high yellow," had dark brown hair and beautiful green eyes. She had large, full breasts and the tightest little booty Reginald had ever seen. She looked exceptionally sexy in a bikini. He was going all out to make sure that this one didn't get away.

Reginald was no longer a member of the football team, but he did manage to make the Dean's List in his first quarter back in school. He was enrolled in four classes, he made three A's and one B. Reginald was now two quarters away from graduating.

"Baby, I'm almost there," Reginald said.

"Well, almost ain't good enough. I want all or nothing," Michele said.

"I know, I know. I am just happy that I could possibly be a college graduate and married to you before you have the baby."

"Well, that's a big *could*. Don't get me wrong, I love you, Reginald. But I am only going to get married once, and I want everything to be right."

Wrong Perception

"I understand, Michele. I am going to finish, just you wait and see."

"I'm not going anywhere. If you finish, I will marry you."

"I love you, Michele."

"I love you, too, Reginald."

Reginald was not as involved with The Gang anymore. He was spending most of his time with Michele, in school or managing his restaurant and laundry mat.

Reginald started attending Lamaze classes with Michele and vowed that he would be the best father in the world. He still kept in frequent contact with his mother, but for some strange reason, he would always seem to play telephone tag with James. Eventually James's mother moved and there was no forwarding phone number available. Reginald no longer made his customary stop at the Jones' during the Christmas holiday season and he became very involved with Michele and what was going on in South Carolina. Reginald would call his father from time to time talking about a possible move back to Atlanta.

"Hey, Daddy."

"Hey, boy. What's going on?"

"Nothing much, just trying to get myself together so I can move back to Atlanta."

"What are you coming back here for?"

"I'm tired of living up here. I'm ready to come home and start working with you, Dad."

"Well, come on. You know I can get you on at the housing authority."

"Yeah I know, that's why I'm calling."

"Well, like I said, come on home. So how is that girlfriend of yours? Is she still holding on to my grandchild?"

"Yep, she's still holding on."

"Well, tell me, are you going to marry this girl?"

"Yep, real soon. When I graduate from college, we are getting married."

"If you have the baby out of wedlock is she going to give the baby your last name?"

"Yeah, she said she was."

"That's all right then, another little Maynard in the world. Do you know if it's going to be a boy or girl?"

James D. Jackson, Ph.D.

"No, not yet, but you will be the first to know."
"Well, let me go, boy, I got some stuff I need to do."
"All right, Daddy, good talking to you."
"Good talking to you, son, good-bye."

12

Broken Promises

After James was released from active duty, he packed up his family and moved to Augusta. On the drive from Fort Stewart to Augusta, James and Heather had a long talk. James made it clear to Heather that she needed to find a job as soon as they got to Augusta and had to keep the job until he graduated.

"I need for you to help support this family for the next two years and after that, you'll never have to work again," James said.

"I heard you the last six times that you explained it to me. I told you that my family means the world to me, don't worry!" Heather said, looking out the window.

"I just wanted you to understand that the kids and I are counting on you to come through for us," James said stressing his point.

"I won't let you down, I promise."

"You better not let us down because this is your last chance. I have been doing everything for you and the kids, now it's your turn to show us that this family is your first priority."

"James, I told you I understand. I won't mess this up, okay?" Heather yelled.

"I hope not," James said, now changing the subject. "You know I think this is going to be the best move we have ever made."

"I hope so," Heather said turning to look out the window.

"Come on, baby, think positive," James said reaching over and grabbing Heather's hand. She couldn't help but smile when she saw the happiness in James's face.

Once in Augusta, Heather started putting in job applications everywhere. After three weeks of looking for a job, Aiken

Regional Hospital offered her a job working in the admissions department. Heather's employer told her that she got the job based on all the medical training that was on her resume.

"Mrs. Jones, by the looks of your resume you have been quite busy over the last few years," the employer said.

"I've tried to keep myself busy, trying to learn everything I could."

"You have a very impressive resume. You are definitely going to be hired. I wish I could find more employees like you."

"Well, my husband paid for all of the training that I received, so I owe my being hired to him."

"Well, you also have a good husband, I wish I could find one like that, too," the employer said as she laughed.

Once James enrolled in his courses, he began studying. By receiving grants and student loans to pay for tuition, James was able to use his GI Bill to pay the rent for their apartment. Heather was responsible for paying the car note, utilities, and buying groceries for the family. The first year worked out okay, James obtained a cumulative grade point average of 3.4, graduated from airborne school and was awarded the superior cadet decoration for being selected as the top ROTC cadet in the junior class. James was also featured in the school's newspaper for being the only cadet in his class who would be receiving a regular Army commission when he returned to active duty. Regular Army commissions are only given to the top five percent of ROTC graduates across the country.

When James returned to Augusta College for his senior year, he told his wife that she only needed to work one more year and she would have proven that she really cared about him, and she would never have to work again.

"Heather, I just want to tell you that I'm proud of you for the support that you have given the family for the past year," James said giving her a hug.

"Thank you, baby," Heather said giving him a hug back.

"Just one more year and we'll be on easy street," James said.

"I know, I know," Heather said rolling her eyes as James held her tighter.

Wrong Perception

Over the summer when James was at airborne school, Heather decided to become friends with some of her coworkers. The three friends that she associated with the most were Brian Oliver, Tanya Franklin and Lisa Smith. In September of 1992, Heather invited Brian and Lisa over to their apartment for a cookout. Heather had previously mentioned to James that Brian was infatuated with her. Quite naturally, James asked why she invited him over to the house if she knew that he was interested in her. Before their guests arrived, they got into another argument about why she invited Brian over to the house if she knew he liked her.

"I can't believe that you invited this guy over to our house. How would you like it if I invited some woman over here that likes me?" James asked, taking the steaks out of the refrigerator.

"I wouldn't mind if it was innocent like the way Brian feels about me," Heather remarked.

"Yeah, you just watch yourself around him," James warned her.

"I don't need to watch myself around him, he's interested in my friend Lisa," Heather said.

Heather continued to try to convince James that Brian's infatuation was innocent and that she was actually trying to set Brian up with Lisa and that was why she invited the both of them over to the house. James was so involved with trying to be a good host that he could not see what was going on right under his nose. James did all of the cooking on the grill. He grilled hamburgers, hot dogs, and steaks. After dinner, Brian and Lisa thanked Heather for inviting them over and they left. A week after the cookout, Tanya called.

"Hello?" Heather said.

"Hey, Heather girl, what's going on?" Tanya asked.

"Oh, nothing girl, just putting my girls down for a nap so I can get some rest," Heather said.

"So, you never told me how the cookout went," Tanya asked.

"It went well," Heather said.

"You mean Lisa and Brian hit it off?" Tanya said surprised.

"Of course they hit it off why wouldn't they?" Heather asked.

"I thought I heard someone say that Lisa was gay," Tanya said.

"You heard right, Lisa is a lesbian," Heather said.

"How did you know she was a lesbian?" Tanya asked.

"Girl, Lisa told me that she was a lesbian," Heather said. She did not know that James was standing right behind her and overheard her comment.

"What in the hell did you just say?" James asked.

"Tanya, I have to go," Heather said, hurrying to hang up the telephone.

"I'll ask you again, what did you just say about Lisa?" James asked.

"I don't know what you're talking about," Heather said, trying to leave the room.

"You're not leaving until you tell me what you told Tanya about Lisa," James said.

"Oh, all right, she is a lesbian," Heather screamed.

"If she's a lesbian, how in the hell were you going to set her up with Brian?" James asked.

Heather stood there with a stupid look on her face. She could not respond, obviously she needed more time to prepare a good lie. Heather told James that she didn't want to talk about it right then and walked away. James told her that he suspected her of having an affair, but she denied it. He told her that having a lesbian friend was an excellent cover up for her relationship with Brian, but Heather continued to deny having any feelings for Brian. In the past, Heather would always tell James that Lisa and Brian were getting along fine, and that she was going over to Brian's house to visit them. Now James was asking why she would do something like this to their family after all they had been through. Heather did not respond. She continued to deny her involvement with Brian and told James that she only cared about her husband and that he had nothing to worry about.

Heather and Tanya worked the night shift together at Aiken Regional Hospital. Since Aiken Regional was a private hospital, during a shift change, money received from the day shift would have to be signed over to the night shift. The night shift would then turn the money over to management in the morning.

Wrong Perception

Heather and Tanya decided that they were going to find a way to beat the system. Working at Aiken Regional Hospital, employees would use their personal identification cards to clock in. If one of the employees was late, only one signature was needed to receive the money from the previous shift for the shift change to occur. As long as two signatures were on the receipt when the collection manager came in the morning, no questions were ever asked. Heather and Tanya decided that if Heather went to work on time, she would take Tanya's I.D. Card with her and clock the both of them in and then Tanya would show up to work about two hours before shift change, or vice versa.

Sometimes one of the two would not go to work at all and the other would have to forge the signatures on the money received document. Heather and Tanya thought they would be able to get away with this illegal act forever because none of the managers worked the night shift. Heather and Tanya were the only two that worked in admissions during the night.

"Heather, I thought you had to work tonight," James asked taking a break from studying.

"No, Tanya said that she had everything under control," Heather said.

"What do you mean Tanya told you she had it under control, she's not your boss," James said.

"Look, Tanya and I know what we are doing," Heather said snapping at James.

"Well, if your ass gets fired from your job, you can forget about this marriage," James snapped back.

"Don't you worry, I know what I'm doing," she said leaving the room. James continued to follow Heather from room to room telling her that it was bad enough that he suspected that she was having an affair, but if she ever got fired from her job for doing something illegal that he would leave her. A week later when the collection manager was reviewing the collections for the month, he noticed an obvious difference in Heather and Tanya's signatures from the previous night. They were called into the manager's office. Heather arrived at the office and saw that Tanya was already in there. Heather walked in and asked Tanya, "Do you know why we were called in here?"

"No, girl, all I was told was that the manager needed to see me," Tanya said. Just then the manager, Mr. Brown, entered the office and sat down without saying a word.

"Mrs. Jones, Ms. Franklin, the two of you were called in today because there is a discrepancy with the signatures on the collection invoices for the last month," Mr. Brown said looking at the both of them. Neither Tanya nor Heather said anything.

"I want the two of you to look at the signatures on the invoices," Mr. Brown said handing the papers to Tanya and Heather. "Now have the two of you been signing for the other?"

Both Heather and Tanya said "yes" at the same time. They were thinking that if they were honest that they would not be punished too severely.

"Well, I'm sorry ladies, but the hospital can not condone such behavior and we're going to have to let the both of you go," Mr. Brown said.

"Mr. Brown, I'm sorry for forging Tanya's signature, but please don't fire me, I need my job, sir."

"I'm sorry, but the two of you should have thought of the consequences beforehand," Mr. Brown said, getting up from his chair to escort the two women out.

"Come on, Heather, let's go," Tanya said as the two headed out the door and to the parking lot.

"So what are you going to do?" Heather asked.

"Girl, I'm going down to the unemployment office and draw my funds," Tanya said laughing.

"What do you find so funny? We're out of a job and I don't know how I'm going to tell my husband," Heather said, now crying because she knew that her marriage was at stake.

"Girl, you've worked for a little over a year at the hospital, you'll be eligible for unemployment. Just tell him that money will still be coming into the house," Tanya said.

"You don't know my husband, he will never understand," Heather said. "Well, let me go and get this over with."

"See ya at the unemployment line," Tanya yelled as she got in her car.

Heather cried all the way home. How in the world was she going to tell James that she lost her job? When Heather reached the apartment, she sat in the car for what seemed like an eternity. She finally got up the nerve to go in the house. James was sitting at the table studying for a biology test when he heard the door close.

"Heather, is that you? I thought you had to work tonight?" James asked.

"Where are the girls?" Heather asked avoiding James's question.

"I asked you a question." James said.

"I heard you the first time," Heather said.

"Well, what are you doing home so early?"

"I got fired, okay," Heather snapped.

"I told you not to do anything stupid, smart ass. Why did you get fired?

"The manager found out that I forged Tanya's signature."

"You had to do it your way. Now your way has cost you me," James said walking away. He knew that he would now have to find a job in the evening after school if he was going to survive. James was able to find a job at the veteran's affairs office filing patient records. He told Heather that he needed some time away for a while to get himself together. James moved in with his friend Kevin Louis in the ROTC department. Kevin was from St. Croix, the Virgin Islands. One Friday afternoon after classes James decided to go by and see his daughters without calling Heather to let her know that he was coming over. When James arrived at the apartment, he went to door and rang the doorbell. Heather answered the door.

"Are the girls at home?" James asked.

"Yes, but why didn't you call first," Heather said. The children heard their father's voice and ran to the door.

"Daddy, Daddy," they yelled as they went running to the door.

"Hey, my two beautiful baby girls," James said as he picked them up.

"Look, James, I have company right now, so you are going to have to leave," Heather said closing the door a little so James couldn't look in.

"So, who's over here?" James asked.

"That's none of your business, you moved out remember," Heather said.

"Yeah, but we are still married," James said raising his voice. Just then Brian came and pulled the door open.

"Is there a problem here?" Brian asked.

"No, Brian, I have everything under control," Heather said. Brian went back inside and waited for Heather.

"James, just leave and next time call before you come over here," Heather said grabbing the girls from him as she closed the door. In January of 1993, James asked Heather if she was not having an affair with Brian to break off her so-called friendship with him. Heather told James she was not giving up her friendship with Brian because nothing was going on between them. A week later, James asked Heather for a divorce. Once he found a lawyer, he called Heather and told her that he had a lawyer that would only cost them one hundred dollars. Heather then informed him that she also had a lawyer that would give them a divorce for one hundred dollars. James had no idea that Heather's lawyer was a friend of Brian's. The divorce decree was written in such a way that James was practically losing everything, and he knew it. He decided to sign the decree so that the nightmare of being married to Heather would finally be over.

James knew that if he stayed around Heather any longer, he would probably be in jail for murdering her. The day after James signed the divorce decree, he decided to purchase a 380 automatic pistol from a local pawn shop. He requisitioned the pistol so that he could start preparing for firing pistols once he returned to active duty. When James bought some ammunition for the pistol, he visited two indoor firing ranges in Augusta. Two weeks later James received a call from Heather.

"Hello," James said answering the phone.

"James this is Heather, I received a check for you in the mail today."

"Okay, I'll be over tomorrow to pick it up," James said.

"Well, I need about sixty dollars of it," she said

"No, I'm not going to be able to give you any money out of that check, I need to get the tags for my car," James said.

"Well, come get it!" Heather said hanging up the telephone in James' ear.

The following day James arrived at Heather's house to pick up the check and noticed that Brian was over at the apartment visiting her.

"What are you doing over here?" Heather asked as Janet and Tammy ran and jumped into their father's arms.

"I just came to pick up my check, remember?"

"Well, I don't have your check, I sent it back to where it came from."

"I told you I was coming over here today to pick it up, and you said okay. Give me my check so I can go."

"I told you, boy, I don't have your goddamn check."

"Look, I don't have time for your games, give me my fucking money."

"Hey, man, she told you she does not have your check. Now get the hell out of here," Brian said.

"Look man, this matter does not concern you."

"Don't tell me what concerns me. If you don't get out of here, I'm going to kick your ass," Brian said.

"I know you are more of a man than to hit a man who is holding his children," James said as he started to put his daughters down.

"I will shoot you and kill you in front of your children, I don't give a fuck about you."

James looked at Heather and said, "Is this the man that you said was supposed to be such a good man?" Heather did not respond, she was enjoying the threats that Brian was making to James.

James walked out of the apartment very upset about what Brian said to him. James walked out into the parking lot and got into his 1990 two door red Pontiac Grand Am. James' 380 automatic was lying on the passenger seat fully loaded. He sat in his car for thirty minutes wondering if he should go back inside the house and shoot Brian.

After contemplating killing Brian, James realized that that was not going to solve anything and drove away. Three days later, Heather mailed James the check. James realized that it was merely a trap to see if he was going to be stupid enough to fight

Brian in her apartment. Heather did not care about the fact that her lie almost got Brian killed. She was only concerned about ruining James' pursuit of becoming a military officer.

After the divorce, James continued to work part time in the medical record section of the VA hospital. He was doing everything he could to keep busy to keep the divorce off his mind. He would study practically every hour he could after class. You could always find him sitting at the picnic table outside the student center between the hours of 12 P.M. and 4 P.M., studying. At 4:30 P.M. he would go to his part-time job and work until 9:30 P.M. This was his routine Monday through Friday. James' classes occupied his days and most of his nights were spent studying, but James was lost without his daughters. He missed combing their hair, giving them their baths, reading them a bedtime story and just talking and playing with them. James loved his daughters more than life itself.

13

The Arrest

One Sunday morning, Reginald received a call from one of the policeman on his payroll. "Hey man, there is a big sting operation about to go down involving The Gang. You better get the fuck out of town, my man," the policeman said.

"Thanks for the heads up, my nigga."

Reginald immediately ran into Stacy's room and informed him of the telephone conversation with the policeman.

"Hey man, we need to get the fuck out of South Carolina, the cops are on to us. We need to leave South Carolina and start a new life in Atlanta," Reginald said.

"You can leave if you want to my nigga, I am staying right here. With your ass out of the picture, I will be the head of The Gang, and that is exactly what I want," Stacy replied.

"You are talking stupid, man. If we don't leave now, we will spend some time in the pen," Reginald said. "We have made more than enough money to last us a long time."

"You must not have heard me, my brother, you can leave, but I am not going anywhere. You had your chance, now it's time for me to take The Gang to the next level. We are going to make more money under my leadership than we ever did under yours," Stacy said.

"Suit yourself you stupid motherfucker. I am getting the hell out of here."

"I'll be in touch," Stacy said sarcastically.

"All right, man," Reginald replied. "I'll be hitting the road in a few minutes my nigga."

An hour later, when Reginald was all packed and ready to go, he made one last plea. "Stacy, you need to pack your shit, man, we need to get out of here."

"I am staying here man, tell your family I said hello," Stacy said.

"You can have the restaurant, my other cars and the money that is tied up in The Gang, I'm out of here," Reginald said as the friends shook hands and Reginald headed out the door and got into his red convertible BMW.

On the three-hour road trip, Reginald had time to think about what had transpired in South Carolina. He recalled the hundreds of people he had gotten hooked on drugs and all the money he made doing it. Reginald was sick to his stomach.

When he arrived in Atlanta, he stopped by his mother's house. When he pulled up in the driveway, his mother was outside watering the grass.

"Hey Mama, I'm home," Reginald said.

"Hey baby, how long are you going to be here?"

"I'm home for good, Mama. I don't have any intention of going back to South Carolina."

"Why the sudden change, baby? Are you in some sort of trouble?"

"No, Mom, I just want to be around my family. I have been gone long enough."

"We are happy to have you home, baby. Where are you going to live?"

"I was hoping I could live with you for a while until I find a job."

"Well you know you can live here as long as you need to, baby. I'm so happy to have you home."

"Thanks, Mom, you have always taken good care of me."

Early Monday morning, Reginald got dressed and headed downtown. He applied for a job at the human resource office to work at one of the Atlanta housing developments where his father was a supervisor.

Two days later, Reginald received a call from the housing development. "Mr. Maynard, my name is Cynthia Wynn, and I work in personnel at the Atlanta Housing Authority. I am calling to see if you can come in for an interview tomorrow."

"Yes, I can, what time do you want me to be there?" Reginald asked.

Wrong Perception

"You need to be here at 10:45 A.M. Our office is located on the second floor of the human resource building where you submitted your application, in room 205," Ms. Wynn said.

"Yes, I know where that is, I will see you tomorrow," Reginald replied.

"Well, okay, we're all set, I will see you tomorrow at 10:45 A.M.," Ms. Wynn said as the two said good-bye.

When he hung up the telephone, Reginald screamed for joy. His other life was finally behind him and he couldn't wait to start his new life. His mother heard him scream and went running into the room to see what was going on.

"What wrong, baby?" Patty said as she ran into the den where Reginald was.

When he saw his mother, he jumped up from the couch where he was sitting, picked his mother up in the air and started swinging her around. He finally put his mother down and gave her a big kiss on the cheek.

"What's gotten into you, Reginald?" Patty asked as she straightened out her dress.

"I have an interview tomorrow—that's what's gotten into me," he said as he flashed his mother his handsome smile.

"I'm proud of you, baby, what time is your interview?"

"I have to be there at 10:45 sharp," Reginald said as he headed to his room to find something to wear.

Reginald stood in front of his closet waiting for an outfit to jump out at him. He had to make a good impression. He wanted to make sure that he did not pick anything too hip-hop or too flashy. He finally decided on his navy suit, a white shirt and a navy and red striped tie. His mother came to his room to get his clothes to press. She wanted her son to look good for his interview. While Patty was ironing Reginald's clothes, he decided to shine his black dress shoes. Patty took Reginald's clothes back to his room and hung them in the closet. He was still shining his shoes when Patty entered his room. He looked up and saw his mother smiling at him.

"I'm going to fix you a big breakfast before you leave for your interview tomorrow, baby," Patty said as she started out the door.

"Thanks, Mom, I would really appreciate that."

"You know I'll do anything for my baby."

"I know Mom, I love you."

"I love you too, baby," Patty said as she exited the room.

Reginald finished his shoes and went to take a shower. When he got out of the shower, his mother and stepfather had already turned in for the night. As Reginald passed their door, he yelled, "Goodnight, Mom and Dad." From behind the door he heard them yell back "Goodnight."

Once Reginald got in his room and closed the door, he collapsed on the bed. His thoughts wondered from his friend Stacy to his girlfriend Michele. Before he knew it, he was dialing Michele's telephone number. After the first ring, Rhonda, Michele's little sister, answered the telephone "Greene's residence, this is Rhonda, how may I help you?"

"Hey kiddo, is your sister there?" Reginald asked.

"Well, if it ain't Mr. Maynard," Rhonda said sarcastically.

"Just put Michele on the phone, would ya," Reginald said getting upset.

Rhonda dropped the telephone on the table and yelled for Michele to pick up. Reginald was calling Rhonda a bitch when Michele answered the telephone. "Hello," Michele said, waiting to hear the voice on the other end.

"Hi, baby, how are you doing?" Reginald asked, now happy to hear Michele's voice.

"I am doing okay. Being pregnant is no easy task," Michele said.

"Well I was just calling you to let you know that I am going for a job interview tomorrow. I think I'm going to get the job because the housing authority needs to hire a lot of people according to my dad," Reginald said.

"Well, good luck with the interview," Michele said.

"Thanks. I was hoping that you would move here and live with me once I get a job."

"Oh, I don't know about that. I have been looking for a job here myself, and remember what I told you, I only want to be with a man who has a college degree," Michele said.

"I know, but I was hoping you would change your mind, seeing that we are going to have a baby and all."

Wrong Perception

"Pregnant or not, I'm not going to be with you, or any other man, unless he has a college degree."

"Well, I'll call you again in the near future to check on you and the baby. I love you very much, Michele, and I hope someday you will change your mind."

"I love you too, Reginald. I'll think long and hard about coming to Atlanta to live with you. I'll let you know in a couple of days."

"All right, you do that. Let me go so I can get some sleep because I have a big day tomorrow," Reginald said.

"Good night, Reginald."

"Good night, Michele."

Tuesday morning, Reginald got up bright and early. He took his shower, put on his clothes and looked in the mirror to make sure everything was in place. When he walked into the kitchen, Patty couldn't help but notice how handsome her son looked in his navy suit.

"Good morning, Mom. Something smells good," Reginald said as he sat down at the table.

"Morning, baby, I cooked you a nice breakfast," Patty said adding the cheese to the eggs.

"Thanks, Mom, you need to make it quick, because I want to get there early."

"Everything's ready," Patty said, placing the plate of food on the table in front of Reginald. Patty made all of her son's breakfast favorites: grits, bacon, cheese eggs and homemade blueberry waffles. She poured two glasses of orange juice and two cups of coffee and joined her son for breakfast.

"Thanks Mom, but I really have to go," Reginald said getting up and kissing his mother on the top of her head.

"Oh, all right, son, good luck with your interview," Patty said as Reginald headed out the door.

The traffic was heavy on the expressway and Reginald was glad that he left early. He turned to his favorite radio station V103.3 FM and enjoyed the sounds of Bobby Brown, Mariah Carey and Whitney Houston as he was on his way downtown.

He arrived at the office at 10:25 A.M. and informed the receptionist that he was there for his 10:45 interview.

"Hello, my name is Reginald Maynard. I am here for my 10:45 interview with Ms. Wynn."

"Please have a seat, sir, I will let Ms. Wynn know that you are here," the receptionist said.

A few minutes later, the receptionist returned. "Mr. Maynard, Ms. Wynn will see you now," she said.

"Mr. Maynard, come on in and have a seat. How are you doing today?" Ms. Wynn asked.

"I'm doing okay, just in desperate need of a job. I have come back to Atlanta, after being away for a few years. I am eager to start working so that I can pay my own way."

"Well, by the looks of your resume, we should be able to find something for you to do. When can you start working?" Ms. Wynn asked.

"I am prepared to work right now, can I start tomorrow?" Reginald asked.

"I don't know why not. I think I know the ideal job for you. I will give you a call at home around four o'clock today to let you know what I have come up with."

"What kind of job do you see me doing?" Reginald asked.

"With your college experience and recommendations, I am looking to start you in the manager's training program," Ms. Wynn said.

Reginald thanked Ms. Wynn as he exited the office. He waited patiently at his mother's house for the telephone call that promptly came at four o'clock.

"Hello?"

"May I speak to Mr. Reginald Maynard, please," Ms. Wynn said.

"This is he."

"This is Ms. Wynn calling to inform you that you got the job, and that I will be looking for you at nine o'clock sharp."

"I will be there, " Reginald said as he hung up the telephone. He was very happy with his new job working forty hours per week. Reginald was thrilled about being back home and around his family.

Meanwhile back in South Carolina, Stacy was working hard trying to make all the money he could. He continued to have the

Wrong Perception

same meetings, stressing to The Gang that they needed to work harder than ever before.

Stacy looked directly at Ramon, one of the members of The Gang. "Look, I am the man in charge now. I am counting on you, Ramon, to be my right hand man. With your knowledge of this area and strong ties to our customers, I intend to pay you more money than you have ever made in your life," Stacy said. "I just want you to remain loyal to The Gang, my nigga."

"Whatever you say, Stacy. You know I have always been loyal to The Gang, because The Gang has been good to me and my family," Ramon replied.

"Ramon, we have a big shipment of cocaine coming in next Thursday. I want you to go with me to pick up the shipment."

"Anything you say, boss, I'm with you," Ramon said.

A large shipment of cocaine with a street value of over three million dollars, was scheduled to be delivered on the following Thursday. Someone tipped off the federal marshals that a large shipment of narcotics was headed to South Carolina. The anonymous person that informed the Marshals gave the date, time and name of the person who would pick up the shipment. The marshals followed up on the anonymous tip and Stacy Mathews was caught red-handed picking up the shipment.

One Saturday morning back in Atlanta, about six weeks later, Reginald was at his parents' home asleep. There was a loud knock at the door. Reginald had moved back to Atlanta to try to get his life back on the right track, but his previous lifestyle had finally caught up with him. Reginald's mother got up from the table where she was enjoying her breakfast to answer the door. A federal marshal asked if she was the mother of Reginald Maynard. She replied that she was. The marshals explained that they had a warrant for her son's arrest and they asked if he was home. Reginald's mother then asked what it was in reference to and the marshals explained that her son would have to stand trial in South Carolina for drug trafficking charges.

Reginald's mother fell to her knees and started crying as she yelled, "God, please don't take my baby away!"

The marshals located Reginald, read him his rights and then they placed him under arrest. Reginald's mother, sister and stepfather stood in the doorway and cried as the marshals drove away with Reginald in custody. While in the car, he was asked about his involvement with The Gang's drug distribution.

"Mr. Maynard, do you care to tell us about your involvement with The Gang?" the marshal riding in the passenger seat asked.

"I don't have a clue to what you are talking about. I have been living in Atlanta for the past three years, so I don't understand how you can say I was involved in anything in South Carolina," Reginald replied emphatically.

The marshal riding in the passenger seat told Reginald, "We have been investigating you for the past three years. We know everything about The Gang and your relationship with them." Once Reginald arrived in South Carolina, the interrogation continued. The interrogating officer, Officer Holmes, used every scare tactic imaginable to get Reginald to confess.

"You better come clean and tell us everything, Mr. Maynard, or you will never see the outside of a prison again. You better give us every name of every person associated with this pathetic organization."

"I don't know what in the hell you are taking about," Reginald said.

"I am going to tell you again, one of my marshals has informed you that we have a star witness that has already come forward and explicitly described your involvement," Officer Holmes said. At that moment, another federal marshal walked by the office where Reginald was being questioned, escorting Stacy Mathews to another part of the building. It finally hit Reginald who the person was that came forward.

"All right Mr. Holmes, I was the head of The Gang for the past few years. I tried to get out of the business of selling narcotics and turn my life around. Obviously, I waited too late," Reginald said sadly.

The federal marshals made it clear to Stacy that he would never see the outside of a prison again if he did not come clean and tell about Reginald Maynard's involvement with narcotics. The deal that was offered to Stacy was that if he ratted on Reginald, he would serve a maximum of six years in the penitentiary. Stacy started singing like a bird, he even brought a few others down with him.

"Reginald was the King Pin of this operation. He intimidated people so bad that he could make a monkey stand on his head if he wanted to. The members of The Gang were so scared of Reginald that they did whatever he said in fear of loosing their lives," Stacy said.

"Mr. Mathews, why did you get involved in The Gang?" Officer Holmes asked.

"I have known Reginald, that son-of-a-bitch, since elementary school. I thought that he was going to take care of things like he always did in the past," Stacy replied.

"What do you mean 'take care of things'?" Officer Holmes asked.

"Well, throughout school Reginald always had his way with the coaches, teachers and girls. I was a bit jealous of that and I always wanted to show him up. I have always wanted to show that motherfucker that I was just as good as he was," Stacy said angrily.

"You know that you are going to spend some time in prison for this?" Officer Holmes asked.

"Yes sir, I fucked up and now it's time to pay," Stacy said nervously.

Reginald and Stacy were sentenced to eight years in the South Carolina State Penitentiary.

14

A New Beginning

Two months after his divorce was final, James became interested in a young lady named Renee Williams. Renee was a student in the sociology department. James and Renee were in the same sociology marketing class and he asked her out on a study date and she accepted. They started to see each other more than just study partners do. A month later, James and Renee started dating seriously. One Friday night, Renee was over at James's apartment and the two had just finished studying for a final when the conversation turned serious. James had told Renee earlier that he loved her and this night she proclaimed her love to him for the first time. The two talked and held each other until ten o'clock that night. James had fallen asleep in Renee's lap when she kissed him on the head waking him up.

"I better be going, I have some relatives coming in from out of town and I need to help my mother clean up the house," Renee said getting up from the sofa.

"When am I going to hear from you?" James asked.

"I'll call you tomorrow, I love you," Renee said as she got her car keys and purse.

"I love you, too," James said laying his head back down on the sofa.

On the way home, Renee was on cloud nine. She sang love songs all the way home. She was ten miles from home, making a left turn on Morgan Road when she was in a car accident. Renee was hit by a drunk driver who ran a red light and smashed into her car, totaling her 1987 four-door Subaru and knocking her unconscious behind the wheel. Eyewitnesses told the police that they thought that the driver of the Subaru was probably dead from the impact of the collision. A man by the name of Frank

James D. Jackson, Ph.D.

Trotter stayed by Renee's side the entire time. He wanted to remove Renee from the smoking car, but the other people who were standing by suggested that he shouldn't because of a potential explosion. An ambulance arrived and Renee was rushed to the Medical College of Georgia Hospital and so was the drunk driver, Eugene Scott. In the emergency room Renee and Eugene were side by side and the police were also there trying to get more information about the accident from them. Renee's mother Mattie and her stepfather Sam arrived shortly after the police called about the accident. Mattie called Pamela, Renee's aunt, to come to the hospital. Mattie and Pamela were by Renee's side in the emergency room while she went in and out of consciousness. The whole time, Eugene was screaming to the top of his lungs "That bitch hit me!" The police had to hit him several times in order to get him to shut up. Renee was immediately taken to the shock trauma treatment wing of the hospital. Other family members were notified by Pamela about the accident and rushed to the hospital to see Renee. After several hours, Renee opened her eyes. Her mother and Aunt Pamela were there when she woke up. She asked her mother and Aunt Pamela what happened and her Aunt Pamela told her. Renee had sustained multiple injuries from the accident. She had several cracked ribs, a concussion, the femur in her right leg was completely broken in half, and she had cuts and bruises on her arms and legs. The next day Renee's only concern was James and her sociology class. She woke up asking for James. Pamela and Renee's cousin Kim remembered where James lived. While Renee's mother stayed with her, Pamela and Kim were off to find James. They found the apartment complex, but didn't know which building James lived in. They saw a young black guy getting out of his car and decided to ask him if he knew James.

"Excuse me do you know a gentleman by the name of James Jones?" Pamela asked.

"Yes, that's my roommate, but he's not home right now. Can I help you?" Kevin said, closing his car door.

"I'm Renee Williams's Aunt Pamela, and this is her cousin Kim. We need to find James. Renee was in a car accident last night," Pamela said, starting to cry.

"Is she going to be okay?" Kevin asked.

"We don't know, she still has to go through surgery," Pamela said.

"Well, follow me, I think I know where to find him," Kevin said getting back into his car. They followed Kevin to Augusta College. James was sitting on the patio of the student center studying. Pamela and Kim explained to James what had happened to Renee.

"James, I don't know if you remember us," Pamela said before James interrupted.

"Yes, your Renee's aunt," James answered.

"Well, this is Renee's cousin Kim, we're sorry to interrupt you, but Renee was in a car accident last night and she's asking for you," Pamela said showing James the pictures of the car.

"Is she all right, where is she?" James asked sliding back into his chair.

"She still has to have surgery on her leg, and the doctors aren't saying much about her status," Pamela said crying.

"What hospital is she in?" James asked.

"She's at the Medical College of Georgia in the shock trauma unit," Kim said. Pamela was crying too hard to tell him herself.

"As soon as I go home and get cleaned up, I'll be up there," James said as he got up and gathered his books. He showed up at the hospital about an hour and a half later. It was there he met most of Renee's family.

The concussion was so severe that Renee did not remember talking to her Aunt Pamela when the family told her about the accident a few weeks later. At the time of the accident, Renee was enrolled in her final sociology class before receiving her degree in sociology with a minor in social work. Renee was not able to attend the classes for the residuum of the quarter, so James made arrangements with their professor, Dr. Case, to take her assignments home to her and help her complete them. James stopped by Renee's house to give her the final for the class.

"Hi Mrs. Johnson, how is our patient today?" James asked Renee's mother as she answered the door.

"Not so good today, maybe seeing you will cheer her up," Mattie said, showing James downstairs to Renee's bedroom.

"You have a visitor," Mattie told Renee as she stepped out of the way revealing James like a present. Mattie went back upstairs so James and Renee could talk.

"Hey, baby, how are you feeling today?" James asked.

"I'm in a lot of pain, James. I feel so miserable," Renee said. "I can't do anything by myself," she said as she started to cry.

"Don't worry, Renee, I'll help you through this."

"I really appreciate that, baby," Renee said as she started wiping her eyes.

"Stop worrying so much about your injuries. Right now, let's concentrate on finishing these last few classes so we can graduate," James said, pulling three sheets of paper out of his book bag.

"What is that?" Renee said trying to sit up in bed.

"It's the final for our sociology class," James said handing Renee the papers.

"Thanks James, I'll get started on this tomorrow," Renee said putting the papers on the other side of the bed. Renee's mother came back to the room and brought them lunch. James and Renee ate lunch, talked and enjoyed each other's company. James had truly changed Renee's mood—she had forgotten all about her pain.

When Renee completed her assignments, James took the assignments back to school and turned them in for her. Renee was able to earn an A in her last sociology class. On August 20, 1993, James graduated from Augusta College with his bachelor's degree in sociology and was commissioned a second lieutenant in the United States Army. Graduating first in his class, he was able to pick and receive the Army branch of his choice with a regular Army commission. James's mother, grandmother, his brother Johnny and daughters Janet and Tammy attended James's special day. Moreover, to his surprise, Renee showed up. She had to walk with the aid of a walker, but he didn't care. He was glad to see her. His family could not have been prouder of James's accomplishment. After the commissioning ceremony was over, James's mother told him that the family was going to treat him to dinner. Renee was meeting his family for the first time. Carolyn had invited Renee and her mother to join them for dinner, but Renee wasn't feeling up to it. James and Renee said their good-byes in the parking lot and went their separate ways.

"Okay, I'm ready, but I need to pick up something first," James said.

"James, what do you need to go and pick up?" his grandmother asked.

"You'll see, just follow me."

"Carolyn, what is James getting now?"

"I don't know, Mama, let's just follow him and see."

After riding in the car with his family, James pulled up on the BMW car lot, got out and headed towards the red 325 convertible.

James's grandmother commented, "That is a very nice car."

"I know, that's why I bought it," James said as he opened the car door and got in.

Coincidentally, the same day that Reginald and Stacy boarded the bus headed to the pen, James was headed to Fort Knox, Kentucky in his red convertible. While at Fort Knox, James would receive his Army officer basic course training.

While at the Army officer basic course, James learned a great deal about modern warfare. He learned how to command a tank platoon and how to apply his leadership in various scenarios. James had a blast at the basic course. He doubled his pay from what it was when he was a Sergeant, and he was very happy about being an officer in the United States Army. He received orders assigning him to Germany, but was able to change his orders with another lieutenant that wanted to go to Germany, because he wanted more time to pursue his relationship with Renee.

James called Renee to tell her the good news. "Renee, it's me."

"Oh, hey, baby, what's going on?"

"I have some good news."

"What's the good news, sexy?"

"I was able to change my orders from Germany to Fort Benning, Georgia," James said. "You know I couldn't be away from you for three years."

"Oh, James, I am so happy," Renee said.

"I am very happy, too. Well, let me go, I just wanted to call you while I was on break to tell you the good news."

During his third month of the course, James went to Augusta and picked Renee up to spend some time with him at Fort Knox. James decided to take Renee to the Post Exchange (P/X) because she wanted to do some Christmas shopping while she was there. While at the P/X James asked Renee to look at some engagement rings at the jewelry counter. Renee looked at one ring in particular and stated, "This is a very pretty ring."

"You really like that ring?" James asked as Renee tried it on.

"Yeah, it's beautiful."

"Well, the ring is not what we came here for, so why don't you look around the store for the things you want." James said. "I will be over in the men's department for a while and I will catch up with you."

"Okay, baby, I'll see you in a few minutes," Renee said.

The moment that Renee was out of sight, James purchased the ring. The two of them met at the women's department and from there decided to go get something to eat. Once they returned to James's room, he started to gather their dirty clothes for the week to wash them while Renee studied for the social services test held in Atlanta. It was while the clothes were on the rinse cycle that James came back to the room and proposed to Renee. While she was reading her book he dropped to one knee beside her and popped the question.

"Renee, I know we haven't being seeing each other long, but I feel in my heart and soul that you are my true soul mate, will you marry me?" James asked nervously showing Renee the ring she tried on at the P/X.

"Yes, I'll marry you," Renee said with tears in her eyes. James kissed her on the lips jumped up and yelled on his way out the door. "I'll be back. I have to put the clothes in the dryer."

Renee was so excited that she called her mother and Aunt Pamela as soon as the door slammed behind James.

The two set their wedding date for June 12, 1994, the day after Renee was to graduate from Augusta College. During the entire time of James and Renee's engagement, Heather tried her best to get James back. He was reassigned to Fort Benning,

Wrong Perception

Georgia on February 15, 1994. When James arrived at Fort Benning, he was assigned to the 3rd Brigade S-4 shop. There were no Armor platoon leader positions available when he arrived at Fort Benning, so his first job was as the Brigade Supply and Services Officer. James performed the job with distinction. He met several people that had a positive impact on his life.

Captain Michael Chatman was assigned as the Brigade S-4 maintenance officer when James arrived. He was also African-American, so he had a special interest in seeing James succeed. He talked to James on a number of occasions about the things that he needed to do or not to do if he wanted to be a successful military officer.

In May of 1994, while assigned to the Brigade S-4 shop, he was able to spend his first rotation as an officer at the National Training Center (NTC) in California. When James was stationed at Fort Stewart as an enlisted soldier, he was deployed five times to the National Training Center. While he was working in the S-4 shop, he learned about how the Army's support elements provide the logistical support for the Combat Arms units. He was at the NTC when he learned that logistics was where his interests were. He was fascinated about how many ways the support units supported the maneuver units. James returned from the NTC on the 10th of June 1994.

On his wedding day, James was very nervous about getting married. He was sure that Renee was the person that he wanted to marry, but he had never had a wedding before and there were over one hundred people scheduled to attend. James wore his Army blue dress uniform on his wedding day. His uniform was highly decorated with medals he earned in the war. At approximately 3:45 P.M., James and Renee were pronounced man and wife. Heather was still trying to convince James that nothing was ever going on between her and Brian all the way up until his wedding day with Renee.

James was not willing to take Heather back because of all the lies, suspected infidelity and the fact that he was now in love with Renee. After realizing that James would not take her back, she decided to marry Brian, since he had been pursuing her all along. Heather and Brian were married in October of the same year.

James D. Jackson, Ph.D.

In September of 1994, James was reassigned to A Company 2-69 Armor where he served as a platoon leader. In October 1994 his unit was deployed to Kuwait as a "show of force" towards the Iraqi Army that threatened to enter Kuwait again. James's mother and wife were at his new unit to see him off. Renee and James's mother cried as the bus pulled off en route to the airport. He spent forty days in the Middle East before returning home. It was a trying time for James being away from his family again.

Once James and the other troops returned home, he was confronted with bad news from his mother that his cousin Calvin had been found dead in a hotel room. This news was devastating to James and his family because Calvin was so young and had a long life ahead of him. His death made James question life.

"What is life really about?" James asked Renee.

"What do you mean, baby?"

"Well, my daughter, and now my cousin, died too young. Why does stuff like this happen?"

"Only the man upstairs knows that," Renee said.

"Yeah, I guess you're right. I tell you what, I better do all the things that I ever wanted to do, because tomorrow is not promised to anyone."

While James was a platoon leader, many of the soldiers in his company that were not in his platoon wanted to be. They would ask if he could try to get them into his platoon because he really cared about soldiers. James would oftentimes take his platoon out for beer after field training exercises. Members of the platoon cared about him so much, that when he would leave late in the evenings to attend meetings, he would have a cooler full of punch waiting for him and his sleeping bag would be laid out when he returned. At his farewell dinner, many of the soldiers cried and made it clear that he was the best platoon leader that they had ever had and that they were going to miss him. After sixteen months of being a platoon leader, James had to interview for the company executive officer job.

"So tell me Lieutenant Jones, why should I select you to be my company executive officer?" Captain Strong asked.

"Because I'm the best man for the job," James responded.

Wrong Perception

"Well, tell me, hotshot, being an executive officer is primarily a job that concentrates on maintenance. Why should I hire you, instead of the other lieutenants applying for the job?" Captain Strong asked.

"Well, the difference between me and the other lieutenants applying for the job is simple. I have been a lower enlisted soldier, I have personally turned the wrenches and changed the oils in vehicles. I have been a sergeant, which means I have taught soldiers how to perform maintenance, and as an officer, I maintained a ninety-six percent operational readiness rate when I was a platoon leader. The other lieutenants have only seen maintenance from the officer's perspective," James said.

"Well, I have five more people to interview so I will get back with all of you in about a week to let you know who I have selected," Captain Strong said.

"Okay sir. Well, thanks for giving me the opportunity to speak with you today," James said as he walked out of the office.

Later that same day, James was being congratulated by the other captains in the battalion for being selected as the next executive officer for Delta Company 2-69 Armor. James was shocked because Captain Strong said that it would be at least a week before he made his decision.

James was reassigned as the Executive Officer for D. Company 2-69 Armor in February of 1996. James decided that he wanted another car and traded his BMW for a Nissan 300 ZX. As the executive officer, he was awarded the "Battalion's Top Gun" trophy for scoring the highest in the battalion on the tank gunnery range. James decided that he had accomplished all of his goals in the Armor Corps, and requested a branch transfer to the Transportation Corps.

In December of 1996, his branch transfer was approved and he was reassigned to the Officer Candidate School as an instructor.

While speaking to his second class of officer candidates, in his opening remarks he stated, "Many people believe that it is very difficult to be successful in life, and I agree, it's no easy task. I have watched many of my closest friends destroy their lives when it appeared that they were destined for greatness. Everyone has the choice in life to do the hard right over the easier wrong. You can have all of the money, power, respect and material things you want, legally. With a little hard work and perseverance, the sky is the limit. You don't have to make excuses or settle for second best. Some people probably doubted you when you told them that you wanted to become an officer, Lord knows they doubted me. As the great motivational speaker Les Brown once said, "Never let someone's negative opinion of you become your reality." When I was a child, I was labeled as learning disabled, but I knew nothing was wrong with me. Now if you think you are going to cruise through this course easily, you are sadly mistaken. However, if you put forth the effort, you will make it, and I will give you my stamp of approval. It is my duty to Officer Candidate School (OCS) and this nation to commission only those that will make this nation proud. Now, your family and close friends are pulling for you and so am I. I do this job day in and day out because of the love I have for helping soldiers. I know I could be doing something different in the civilian world, but right now, I am happy to be serving my country. Are there any questions?"

"Lieutenant Jones, what do you expect from us?" one of the candidates asked.

"Well, looking at some of your records, many of you already know what it means to be professional. For those of you that don't know, I expect you to present yourselves as men and women with integrity. I expect you to study hard for your exams and follow all of the rules and regulations of OCS. As Norman Vincent Peale once said, 'A would-be achiever must believe in himself or herself, have confidence in one's ability and goals. The achiever must believe in other people, for without helping hands no ladder can be climbed. One must also believe in the country, which affords opportunity, and be a believer in opportunity itself. Anyone who wants to advance must believe in the organization where he or she is employed. And all belief should be undergirded by a solid trust in the help of God.'"

While assigned to OCS, James produced the best platoon in the company for each of the two 14-week cycles that he instructed.

Wrong Perception

In the spring of 1997, James enrolled in Troy State University's Master's of Education degree program. He was accepted after passing his entrance exam and for possessing the mandatory undergraduate 2.5 GPA. He was highly motivated and excited about pursuing a master's degree. James was still assigned to the Officer Candidate School when he was attending night school classes at Troy State. He took two classes during his first term, Foundations of Education and Educational Psychology.

"Dr. White, why is there so much emphasis placed on child abuse nowadays?" James asked.

"You will learn in Educational Psychology that most of the hard-core criminals in the United States were abused in one way or another," Dr. White said. "Violence is not the answer. Parents who abuse children need to get some psychiatric help.

"Dr. White, what is your opinion on spanking children?" James asked.

"Spanking children is okay. So many parents start off spanking their children, but go overboard and seriously hurt the child. That's why authorities are cracking down on parents spanking their children because too many parents are starting to go overboard. Years ago, many parents spanked their kids as a form of discipline and it seemed to be an effective way of changing bad behavior. You have to understand, Mr. Jones, that spanking and child abuse are two different things. Child abuse is when you hit or spank a child that has done nothing wrong. Spankings are given to change bad behavior. Abuse can create mental or emotional problems, whereas spankings are intended to change unwanted behavior. Why do you ask, Mr. Jones?"

"No particular reason, I was just wondering what effect abuse will have on a child later in life," James asked.

"Well, the statistics show that if abuse is done repeatedly, the child will either be very withdrawn or become very violent. Have you ever heard the cliché, violence perpetuates violence?" Dr. White asked.

"Yes, I have," James responded.

At the end of the quarter, James was able to make two A's in his classes.

James D. Jackson, Ph.D.

In his second term he decided to enroll in four courses where he made two A's and two B's. In his final quarter he again took four classes and made three A's and one B, graduating with a 3.7 GPA. During his studies in the master's degree program, James learned that physical abuse of children can leave long-term emotional scars on them.

Whenever James' daughters visited with him, he would always ask if they were okay. He would sit down and have a talk with his daughters about physical abuse. In addition, he would ensure that no pervert was making sexual advances toward his daughters. James would explain that if a man put his hand on their private parts, it was wrong and that they should tell him if that ever happened.

"You two must understand something."

"What's that, Daddy?" Janet asked.

"You did not ask to be in this world. It was a conscious decision between your mother and I to bring you into this world."

"What are you trying to tell us, Dad?" Janet asked.

"My job as a parent is to prepare you for the world. I mean, I should read to you all the time, teach you how to do math and the other subjects, spend quality time taking you places, but more importantly, teach you about life. I don't want to ever spank you, but I will if you get out of line."

"Did Grandmother Carolyn use to spank you, Daddy?" Janet asked.

"She beat me all the time. She would hit me so hard sometimes that I thought I would die. I thought my mother hated me."

"Why did you think she hated you, Daddy?" Janet asked.

"I thought that she spanked me because she hated me. I now understand that being a parent is hard work. Your grandmother did what she thought was best for me, and God knows I gave your grandmother problems growing up. She always whipped me when I did something wrong, never out of hate or just being mean. I am happy she did what she did because I am alive and well and able to take care of you two. It was hard raising four children practically by herself. I love my mother dearly, and thank God every day for my being born to such a caring individual."

The 2nd of September 1997 was a very proud day for James. Not only was he promoted to the rank of captain, but his younger brother Jeff called him to let him know that he had just completed the paperwork that made Jeff the co-owner of two car dealerships. James really wanted Jeff to be at his promotion ceremony, but he understood that it was also a big day for his brother.

James held his promotion in the Officer Candidate School Hall of Fame. He had acquired so many friends that the room was packed during the ceremony. James' mother, stepfather, grandmother, father-in-law, mother-in-law and wife attended.

"I would like to say thank you to everyone who has come out to support me on this special day. I would like to thank God above. Through him all things are possible."

After James graduated from the Officer Advanced Course and the Combined Arms Services Staff School, he requested that he be reassigned to Fort Stewart, Georgia.

When James arrived at Fort Stewart in December of 1998 he began serving as the Transportation Officer for the 87th Corps Support Battalion. He was very excited about moving to Savannah and being close to his brother Jeff. James bought a beautiful three-bedroom house and acquired several mutual funds, money market accounts and an IRA. Two days prior to going home for Thanksgiving Day, James enrolled at Georgia Southern University to complete his doctorate degree in management.

When James arrived at his mother's house on the day before Thanksgiving, Johnny invited him to work out at the gym.

"Hey, James, Jeff and I are going to the gym, do you want to go?" Johnny asked.

"Sure, man, let me go upstairs and change clothes, and I will be right with you."

When James returned downstairs and started lacing up his tennis shoes, he asked Jeff if he could help him get a bigger car.

"Hey Jeff, I want a big fancy car this time."

"Okay, so what are you trying to tell me?"

"Well, I will be moving closer to my daughters now, so the two-seated 300ZX is not going to cut it anymore."

"Well, what kind of car do you want, big money grip?"

"Oh, no, you are the one with all of the big money."

"Well, tell me, what kind of car do you want?"

"Oh, I don't know. I'm tired of seeing the 525 BMW and the 300 Mercedes."

"Well, how about a Lexus for Renee and a Toyota Camry for you?"

"Oh James, the Lexus and the Camry are very nice cars," Carolyn said. "I really like the white Lexus GS300."

"Well Jeff, can you find me one of those?"

"I know exactly where to get one."

With the help of his brother, James traded in his Nissan 300ZX for a pearl white Lexus GS300 and a silver Toyota Camry.

During the Christmas holiday season, James was upstairs in his mother's house working on the computer, when the telephone rang. Carolyn answered the telephone and to her surprise, it was a call from the South Carolina Penitentiary asking if she would accept a call from Reginald Maynard, and she said yes.

"Mrs. Jones, is that you?" Reginald asked.

"Yes it is."

"This is Reginald Maynard, is James around?"

"Yes, he is, it's so good to hear your voice. Hold on a minute."

"James, telephone!" Carolyn yelled.

"I got it, Mom," James replied. "Hello?"

"Hey, James, it's me, Reginald Maynard. I got your mom's new phone number from a guy who came to visit me and says he knows your mother."

"Where are you man?"

"I know you knew I went to prison, right?"

"No, I didn't. I'm sorry to hear it. How long have you been in prison?"

"I have been in here since August of '93."

"How did you wind up in there?"

"I was arrested for selling drugs."

Wrong Perception

"Well, what do you do everyday?"

"I was lifting weights a lot, but some stupid new plan from Congress or some damn where says prisoners can't work out with weights anymore," Reginald said. "How about you, I heard you got married and joined the Army. Are you a sergeant yet?"

"I used to be a sergeant, now I'm a captain."

"Get the fuck out of here. You, a captain?"

"Yeah man, I was promoted back in September."

Reginald hesitated and said, "That's great man, that's great."

James hearing the hesitation in Reginald's voice asked, "What's wrong, man?"

"Oh nothing, I'm proud of you. Really I am. It's just that being in a place like this, I've had a lot of time to think. I often reminisce about our younger days. Did you know I was voted most likely to succeed?"

"Yeah, I knew that."

"The only thing I succeeded at was ruining my life. I am very proud of you, James. As destructive and as bad as your ass was growing up, you are the one that became successful. It's like some kind of wrong perception or something."

"What do you mean by 'wrong perception'?"

"I mean the same thing as crossroads, interchange, or let's say, changing places. Who would have ever thought that your bad ass would become so successful, and I would be the one to wind up in here."

"Reginald, how's your family doing?" James asked to change the subject.

"Well, you know my real dad has been sick a lot. I hear it's his liver, probably from all of the drinking he did years ago. Mom is still taking this incarceration shit pretty hard. Monique is still dating that same girl I told you worked for my father years ago. She is talking about going to Hawaii so that they can get married. In Hawaii, lesbians and faggots can get married, you know?"

"No, I didn't know that," James said.

"So how are your brothers and sister doing?"

"Jeff owns two car dealerships."

"Get the hell out of here."

"Yeah, he owns one in Savannah and one in Vidalia, Georgia.

"How about Johnny, what is he doing now?"

"He graduated from the University of Georgia and joined the Army. He's a helicopter pilot in the Army."

"Hell, no. How about Gina, how is she doing?"

"When she graduated from college, she accepted a job as a marketing director for Sears."

"Get out of here."

"Yeah man, Gina is doing pretty good. Tell me Reginald, did you ever have any children?"

"Yeah, a little boy. As a matter a fact, I named my little boy after you."

"What made you decide to do that?"

"Well, when I got my stupid ass locked up, all I could think about was that conversation we had when I came to visit you at Alabama State."

"I'm flattered that you would name your son after me. Thanks man, that means a lot to me."

"Well, he's living with his mama here in South Carolina. They have come to visit me here a few times. How about you, do you have any crumb snatchers?"

"Yeah, I have two little girls, Janet and Tammy," James said proudly. "What ever happened to Stacy Mathews?"

"I don't care to talk about that punk ass mama's boy. That sell out motherfucker is the reason I'm in here. I tried to get out of the business by moving back to Atlanta, but Stacy with his dumb ass thought that he should stay and run things. After I moved back home, Stacy got caught picking up drugs in South Carolina and brought me down with him."

"Well when are you getting out?"

"I don't know for sure, but I'm up for parole in two years. Hey, James man, I have to go. This damn prison guard is telling me my time is up."

"Well all right, man. Call my mother back when you get a chance and leave your address, so I can write you."

"I can do that. Be good and tell the family I said hello."

"You know I will. I love you, man."

"I love you too James, good-bye."

Wrong Perception

Reginald, James, and Stacy are not the friends that they once were. Hopefully, in time, their friendship will be restored. This story is proof that even when our family, friends, and educators think that they can perceive what our paths will be, they oftentimes have the wrong perception. Don't let anything or anyone set boundaries on you.

No limits!

About the Author

Dr. James D. Jackson is a Healthcare Representative with U.S. Pharmaceuticals Group - Pfizer Incorporated. He holds an Associates degree in Computer Science, a Bachelor of Science degree in Liberal Studies, a Bachelor of Arts degree in Sociology, a Master of Science degree in Education and a Doctorate degree in Management.

Dr. Jackson also served as a sergeant in the United States Army during Operation Desert Shield/Desert Storm and was highly decorated for his contributions during the war. He completed his military service after earning the rank of captain. He resides with his wife in Lakeland, Florida and is currently working on his second book entitled, *Generations to Follow*.

For more information about Dr. James D. Jackson and *Wrong Perception*, visit http://www.wrongperception.com